Something's FISHY, HAZEL GREEN

Also by ODO HIRSCH

Hazel Green
Bartlett and the Ice Voyage
Bartlett and the City of Flames
Bartlett and the Forest of Plenty

Something's FISHY, HAZEL GREEN

by

ODO HIRSCH

Copyright © 2000 by Odo Hirsch
First published in Australia in 2000 by Allen & Unwin
First published in Great Britain in 2001 by Bloomsbury Publishing

Published by Bloomsbury Publishing, New York, London, and Berlin
Distributed to the trade by Holtzbrinck Publishers

Library of Congress Cataloging-in-Publication Data
Hirsch, Odo.
Something's fishy, Hazel Green / by Odo Hirsch.
p. cm.
First published in Australia by Allen & Unwin, 2000.
The Children's Book Council of Australia short-listed book.
Summary: As Hazel tries to find out who took two lobsters from Mr. Petrusca's fish shop, she
discovers that the fishmonger has a secret and determines to help him.
ISBN-10: 1-58234-928-2 • ISBN-13: 978-1-58234-928-2
[1. Secrets—Fiction. 2. Reading—Fiction. 3. Lobsters—Fiction. 4. Interpersonal relations—
Fiction. 5. City and town life—Australia—Fiction. 6. Australia—Fiction.
7. Mystery and detective stories.] I. Title.
PZ7.H59793So 2005   [Fic]—dc22   2004062698

First U.S. Edition 2005
Printed in the U.S.A.
1 3 5 7 9 10 8 6 4 2

Bloomsbury Publishing, Children's Books, U.S.A.
175 Fifth Avenue, New York, NY 10010

All papers used by Bloomsbury Publishing are natural, recyclable products
made from wood grown in well-managed forests. The manufacturing processes
conform to the environmental regulations of the country of origin.

1

HAZEL GREEN LOOKED down from her balcony. It was early, much earlier than she had ever been up before. The springtime sun had come streaming between the curtains in her bedroom and headed straight for her face, like a warm feather duster tickling her nose, like a golden voice humming in her ear. And what was it humming? That a new, fresh day was ready to start. And the sooner she got up, the sooner it would begin.

Out on the balcony, the railing was wet with dew. The tiles under Hazel's bare feet were cool. The air was still chilly from the night. Hazel pulled her dressing gown snug around her. Twelve storeys below, the street was empty. A bird twittered. Its voice was clear and pure. It warbled, stopped, and warbled again, as if it were so early that not even the birds were sure whether they should start singing yet. Hazel listened. The chilly air made her skin tingle, and the chirping song of the birds made her smile, and the empty street made her happy, because everything she could see from her balcony, the whole city, was *hers*, and there wasn't anyone else to share it . . .

There wasn't anyone else . . .

There wasn't . . .

Yes—there was!

Hazel frowned. She could hear an engine. The bird had stopped singing, as if it were listening as well, as if it were thinking exactly what Hazel was thinking, which was: What was anyone doing driving around at this time of the morning? In fact, if people were going to drive around this early, there was hardly any point in getting up. It ruined everything!

Hazel leaned forward over the railing. Nothing. The street was empty for as far as she could see. The noise stopped. There was silence for a moment. Then it started again, a deep, raw rumble, a rusty, throaty roar. Getting louder . . . Coming closer . . .

A van appeared at a corner. Hazel watched it. The van stopped, waited, then started moving again, turning left and rumbling towards her.

It was a grey van. Its body was big and square, and it had a small, narrow snout. It came slowly and steadily along the road, just like a mouse creeping, whiffling and sniffling. A mouse, thought Hazel, with a bad cold and a nasty, rumbling cough.

The van crept past beneath her. Then it pulled in and stopped.

The noise of the engine died. A door opened. Hazel watched to see who would get out. It was a man in a dark shirt and a long white apron. What was he doing all by himself so early in the morning? If he was up to no good, Hazel suddenly realised, she would be the only witness!

The man went around to the back of the van to open the doors. Hazel peered closer to see who it was. Suddenly her eyes went wide.

It was Mr Petrusca, the fishmonger!

By the time Hazel reached the street, after running down twelve flights of stairs, both doors of the van were open. Mr Petrusca was leaning into it. When he turned around he was carrying an enormous crate.

'Hello,' said Hazel.

Mr Petrusca gave a start. 'Hazel! Where did you come from?'

Hazel frowned. That depended where you wanted to start and how far back you wanted to go.

'I saw you from my balcony,' said Hazel. 'But I heard you even before that.'

Mr Petrusca was confused. 'You heard me?'

'Is that crate heavy?' asked Hazel. It looked heavy. It was full of fish and ice.

Mr Petrusca nodded. His arms were straining to carry it. He took it inside. Hazel waited beside the van until he came back.

'What are you doing, Mr Petrusca?'

'What does it look like, Hazel? I'm unloading my van.'

Mr Petrusca leaned in and pulled out another crate of

fish. He carried it towards his shop.

'Did you load it yourself?' said Hazel, following him in.

'Of course,' said Mr Petrusca. He set the crate down at the back of his shop, behind the counters. Hazel followed him as he went out to the van again.

'That seems like a lot of work,' said Hazel.

'It is,' called out Mr Petrusca, with his head in the van. He pulled out another crate. 'But how else are the fish going to get here? Do you think they can walk by themselves?'

Of course not, thought Hazel. That was ridiculous! Fish can't walk.

'And they don't swim here either,' said Mr Petrusca, as if he knew exactly what Hazel was thinking. 'I go and get them, that's how!'

Hazel followed Mr Petrusca into the shop again. 'Where do you get them?'

'From the fish market.' Mr Petrusca dumped the crate on the ground. 'Didn't you know?'

No, Hazel didn't know.

Mr Petrusca folded his arms across his chest. He had cloudy blue eyes, so soft and gentle that sometimes it was hard to believe they belonged to the same person whose thick red hands could slit, gut and fillet a fish in less than a minute, and now they gazed at Hazel with puzzlement, as if he couldn't quite believe that here, right in front of him, close enough to touch, in flesh and blood . . . was a person who didn't know about the fish market!

'Behind the docks, Hazel, there's an enormous market, as big as a football field. All the fishermen bring their catch in the mornings. It opens at two and it closes by five, and in that time they sell everything they've caught. Don't ask me how many fish that makes. Thousands. More. Thousands and thousands.'

'And prawns?' said Hazel.

Mr Petrusca nodded.

'And oysters?'

'Oysters as well.'

Hazel glanced at the crates of fish lying around her. 'And you go every day?'

'Of course!' said Mr Petrusca. 'Don't you think my fish are fresh?'

'Oh yes,' said Hazel quickly. Telling a fishmonger his fish weren't fresh was probably the nastiest thing you could do. It would make him want to slit and fillet *you*. Besides, Mr Petrusca's fish *were* fresh, everybody said so. 'It's just that . . .'

'What?'

'I didn't know,' said Hazel.

Mr Petrusca chuckled. 'You have to be up early, Hazel. The best and the freshest fish are sold at once. And if I can't give my customers the best and the freshest, I'd prefer to give them nothing at all.'

'I *am* up early. I'm up earlier than anybody.'

'Not early enough for me,' said Mr Petrusca, and he went back out to the van, laughing to himself.

Hazel frowned. She gazed at the crates on the floor around her. There were already ten or eleven that Mr Petrusca had brought in. There was a shallow crate of brown horny crabs, crawling and sliding over each other, snapping their claws. Next to them was a box full of salmon. They were as long as your arm and Hazel could imagine the way their lovely pink flesh would taste if you cooked them just right. Hazel's mother always cooked a whole salmon whenever there was a special occasion, like her grandmother's seventieth birthday. There must have been a dozen salmon in the box. Hazel wondered whether there were a dozen families having special occasions that day. Of course, it was possible, because there were a lot of grandmothers around, she knew, and since they were so old, they were often turning seventy, or even eighty.

Beside the salmon was a box of big, flat fish. These ones had both eyes on the same side of their heads, which didn't seem right, at least for a fish. Then there was a crate of shiny mussels, with beardlets of bright green seaweed clinging to their shells. Then there was a tray of squid, with straglets of tentacles and shivery white bodies. Then there was a tray of prawns, with streamlets of legs and eyes like tiny black berries. Next to them was a box of sardines which were no bigger than your finger. Then there was a big box of eels, that looked just like snakes, but slimy and sticky instead. And then there were boxes of other fish mixed together, grey and yellow and red and silver and bluish and all the other colours that a fish can be, and some of them had fins with sharp spines, and some of them had long snouts with teeth, and some of them had little whiskery things near their mouths, and some of them had big humps on their back, or spots on their skin, or freckles on their nose, or stripes on their sides . . .

Yet it wasn't about the fish that Hazel was thinking, it was about one simple fact: *she didn't know*.

Ever since she was a little girl Hazel had lived in the Moodey Building, where the whole ground floor was taken up with shops of one sort or another, and she knew almost all the shopkeepers. By now she thought she had discovered everything about them. For instance, she knew how the baker, Mr Volio, and his assistants, baked all night and finished their work just when everybody else was getting up in the morning. And she knew how the fruiterers, the Coughlins, stored their fruit and vegetables in two big storerooms behind their shop, and had a third storeroom which they only used for extra big deliveries of potatoes. And she knew how Mr Petrusca could slit, gut and fillet a fish in fifteen seconds, and open an oyster with his flat oyster knife in the blink of an eye.

Yet all these years—all these years that she had been coming to visit the fishmonger and Mr Petrusca would smile at her as he filleted fish for his customers—he had been getting up at two in the morning and going to the giant market behind the dock before she was even awake . . . and she had no idea!

And what was even worse was that, if only she had bothered to think, she would have known that *something* was going on. After all, how *did* the fish get to Mr Petrusca's shop every day, if it wasn't Mr Petrusca who went and got them?

Mr Petrusca was still coming in and out with boxes. The last one contained big fish with bright silver bellies and striped blue backs. And finally he came in hauling the tail half of an enormous fish that would have been as big as Hazel herself—perhaps bigger—when it was whole. He was carrying it over his shoulder, grasping it by both hands around the tail. Hazel could see the rich, dark flesh where it had been cut.

Mr Petrusca lowered the half-fish onto the counter, and then he arched his back, to stretch his muscles after all that carrying. There were boxes of fish all around him.

'Well, what do you think, Hazel?'

'They look fresh, Mr Petrusca, that's for sure!'

Mr Petrusca grinned. 'Come here, Hazel. Now I'll show you something really special.'

They went back out to the van. There was only one box

left. This one had a lid. Mr Petrusca lifted it and carried it inside. He put it down on the counter. Then, very carefully, he opened it.

Hazel peered into the box. Inside were two lobsters. They were easily the biggest lobsters Hazel had ever seen.

'Are they dead?' asked Hazel, poking a finger at one of them. It jumped and started thrashing as soon as she touched its shell. An instant later the other one was jumping with it. Hazel only just got her finger away from their snappers in time!

Mr Petrusca laughed. 'I don't think they liked that! Come on, let's put them in the tank.'

In the front of the shop there was already a tank of lobsters waiting to be sold. None of them was anywhere near as big as the two enormous lobsters in the box. Mr Petrusca went into the back of the shop, where there was a second tank. It was filled with water but there was nothing else in it. Very carefully, he took each lobster out and placed it on the glass at the bottom.

Immediately the lobsters came to life. They jumped, crawled and set off around the tank, waving their claws in the water. They bumped and clashed with each other and set off around the tank again, until they bumped and clashed once more.

'Each of these lobsters,' said Mr Petrusca as they watched, 'was like a king in his part of the sea, Hazel. They ruled the sand. Look at the size of them. They're probably twenty years old.' Mr Petrusca stared at the lobsters silently for a while. Their shells, like the armour of knights in ancient times, were knobbly with age. 'I didn't get them both from the same fisherman. Oh no, you'd never find such big ones living near each other. In fact, I've never found two at the fish market on the same day before. Normally, I have to search for weeks to find a pair.'

A pair? Why did he need a pair?

'They're for Mr Trimbel. He's one of my oldest customers. Every year he asks me for a pair of the biggest, most succulent lobsters I can find. It's for a special lobster dinner that he always has with a friend. This is the thirtieth year, Hazel. Imagine that! And this year I think I've found him the best ever.'

They watched the lobsters, which had stopped thrashing now and had come to rest at opposite ends of the tank, eyeing each other suspiciously.

'The best ever,' murmured Mr Petrusca. 'If I feed them carefully, they may get even bigger.'

2

MR PETRUSCA DID feed them carefully. He gave the lobsters everything he could think of that a lobster might like. Bits of sardine, and pieces of crab. He rang up other fishmongers to see what they suggested and spoke to the fishermen at the fish market each day. Someone recalled hearing that sea urchin was good. Someone else remembered an old fishermen who once said that Barbary squid was the best. Sea urchin and squid went into the tank. Mr Petrusca didn't stop to think how much it all cost. He didn't care. Mr Trimbel had been coming to him for thirty years, and if he couldn't provide the biggest, juiciest lobsters after all that time, his name wasn't Petrusca, Fishmonger of Distinction!

'But your name *is* Petrusca, Fishmonger of Distinction,' Mrs Petrusca would say, 'and you don't need to make those lobsters even bigger to prove it.'

Mr Petrusca would grin, winking at Hazel, who sometimes came into the shop after school to see what was happening with the lobsters. As soon as Mrs Petrusca had gone back to the front of the shop, where a customer was waiting, he would whisper: 'So, what do you think, Hazel, are they getting bigger? They are, aren't they?'

Hazel couldn't say. Personally, she doubted that a lobster could grow any more if it was already twenty years old. They must stop growing some time! But people were likely to see whatever they want to see, as her grandmother often said, and Mr Petrusca *wanted* to see the two lobsters growing bigger, heavier and juicier by the day.

'Why don't you weigh them?' Hazel asked. 'Then you'd know for sure.'

'It's terribly hard to weigh lobsters,' replied Mr Petrusca, 'they thrash around all the time.'

'But I've seen you weigh others,' said Hazel.

'And have you seen them thrash?'

'Fish thrash as well, and you weigh them!'

Mr Petrusca stared at Hazel. A fishmonger didn't need to be told that fish thrash. He spent half his life with fish thrashing around him.

'It's hard to weigh them *accurately* when they're thrashing,' Mr Petrusca said at last.

Hazel smiled. Really, Mr Petrusca! It sounded as if he didn't want to weigh them just in case he discovered they weren't growing. Besides, even if the scales showed that they *were* getting bigger, Hazel doubted they could ever grow as much in reality as they were growing in his imagination.

'It might only be a couple of grams,' said Mr Petrusca, who didn't sound as if he believed the explanation himself. 'They might only be a couple of grams bigger. You'd never pick up a couple of grams with the lobster thrashing on the scale.'

'No,' said Hazel.

'You wouldn't, Hazel. Really!'

'Of course not,' said Hazel, turning back to look at the tank. The giant lobsters crawled around each other in the water, slipping over the bottom of the tank with their legs whirring like the oars of a boat, their antennae swirling around their heads, their claws waving in the water, each one a king forced to share his kingdom with another.

'I don't think he's even going to give those lobsters to Mr Trimbel,' Hazel said to Mrs Gluck, who had the flower shop on the ground floor. 'Do you know what I think, Mrs Gluck? I think he loves them so much he's going to keep them for ever!'

Mrs Gluck didn't reply. She was working on an arrangement for the twentieth wedding anniversary of one of her customers, Mrs Margoulis. Mrs Margoulis always wore bright silk scarves and most of them were decorated with flowers. Mrs Gluck had tried to match the bouquet to Mrs Margoulis's favourite scarf. There were yellow rosebuds, pale lemon lilies and bright orange tulips, all nestling in a bed of leaves.

Mrs Gluck's hands whirred round and round the stems, tightening the twine. They moved faster than the eye could follow. Marcus Bunn, who had come to visit her with Hazel, gazed in fascination. Marcus wore spectacles with gold frames and his cheeks were always shiny and red, as if he had just come in out of the snow. Of course, Marcus would never have admitted that he liked coming with Hazel to visit the workroom at the back of the flower shop, which was no place for a *boy*, but somehow he always seemed to forget about that as soon as Mrs Gluck selected a set of blooms and began to weave the colours skilfully into one of her beautiful arrangements. For that matter, Marcus probably wouldn't have admitted how much he liked Hazel Green, either, even though he liked her more than any other girl, more than *anyone*, in fact, even though Hazel was the most unpredictable person he knew and he could never be sure exactly what she was going to say to him from one moment to the next.

Mrs Gluck glanced at him as she finished the arrangement. Marcus tried to put on a frown, as if to say that the arrangement wasn't *that* interesting, not to a boy, anyway.

Mrs Gluck smiled.

'He keeps feeding them and feeding them,' said Hazel. She leaned her elbows amongst the leaves and cuttings on Mrs Gluck's worktable, and rested her chin in her hands. 'He'll never let them go. They're the most magnificent lobsters he's ever seen. That's what he says, Mrs Gluck. The *most* magnificent lobsters.'

'He'll let them go,' said Mrs Gluck quietly, looking at her order book.

Hazel sat up sharply. 'Why? How do you know?'

'What else are they for, Hazel? Think about it. Mr Petrusca is a fishmonger. What makes him proud is to give the best fish to his customers. It doesn't make him proud to have a big lobster in the back of his shop—it makes him proud to be able to give it to someone, and not just *anyone*, but a customer who'll really appreciate it.'

'*I'd* appreciate it!' said Marcus.

'Rubbish,' said Hazel. 'What would you do with it?'

'I'd . . . cook it.'

'Cook it? Marcus, your mother doesn't even let you boil a kettle.'

'I'd cook it . . . and then I'd give it to you, Hazel.'

Hazel shook her head. That wasn't going to work. 'The day I'd eat anything you cook, Marcus Bunn, would be the day before I starve to death.'

Marcus smiled. At least she'd eat it then. Knowing Hazel, it was just as likely she would have said she'd prefer to die.

'No, on the other hand, I'd prefer to die.'

Mrs Gluck was already collecting the flowers for her next bouquet. Hazel watched her. Maybe Mrs Gluck was right. Mr Volio, the baker, was always happiest when watching a customer eating one of his scrumptious pastries. When Hazel ate one of his Chocolate Dippers, for instance, he beamed with pleasure. But he wouldn't be proud of them if they just sat on a tray in the back of his shop, no matter how scrumptious they were. There just wouldn't be any point to them.

'Look at these flowers, Hazel,' said Mrs Gluck, extending her arms. All around her, the workroom was bursting with colour. Blooms flared in vases and buckets, yellow, blue, red, purple, green, orange, pink, white and all the shades in between. 'Look at these colours. And not just the colours. Look at the shapes. Smell the perfumes.'

Mrs Gluck picked up a pair of luscious crimson roses. Their redness was so rich and bright that it seemed to flood out of them, sucking you into a pool of colour. Their perfume drenched the air.

'These are the best I can find, Hazel. My flowers are always the best I can find. Why? Do you think they would give me a moment's pleasure if I kept them here all to myself until they withered away? Even if I could cast some kind of magic spell so none of the flowers in this room would ever die, as long as I kept them all . . . do you think I would ever come back here to look at them? They're not for me. They're for my customers. They're for people who come to my shop for flowers because they appreciate them.'

'I'd appreciate them,' Marcus whispered to Hazel.

Hazel nodded—not at Marcus, but at Mrs Gluck. That's what they were for. That's what Mr Volio's

Chocolate Dippers were for. And that's what Mr Petrusca's lobsters were for.

'Come on,' said Hazel, 'let's go.'

Marcus looked up with a start.

'You don't want to watch Mrs Gluck arrange *flowers*, do you?'

'Of course not,' spluttered Marcus, getting to his feet.

'Marcus,' said Mrs Gluck, 'do you know what this flower is called?'

Marcus turned quickly to look. Mrs Gluck was holding the stem of a purple tulip, so dark that it was almost black.

Marcus shook his head, gazing at the flower in fascination.

'Queen of the Night,' said Mrs Gluck, 'the darkest tulip there is!'

'Do you think I could see these lobsters?' said Marcus, when they had left Mrs Gluck's shop and were walking back towards the entrance of the Moodey Building.

Hazel stopped and looked at Marcus, as if considering whether a boy like him could possibly be allowed to see a pair of prize lobsters that were being fed on sea urchin and Barbary squid.

'All right,' she said after a moment, 'but you'll have to be very quiet, because the lobsters are growing, and every noise disturbs them.'

'Really?' said Marcus.

No, thought Hazel. Why should a noise disturb a growing lobster more than any other?

'Come on,' she said.

'Now?' asked Marcus.

'Why not? Do you think you have to make appointments with a lobster?'

'Can you wait five minutes? I'll just try to find Mandy Furstow. She'd like me to take her to see them.'

'*You* take her to see them?'

'Well . . . if *we* take her . . . I mean . . .'

Marcus stopped. Hazel was looking at him sternly.

'On second thoughts, Mandy doesn't need to come.'

But for all the difference it would have made, they might just as well have waited for Mandy—and for anyone else that Marcus wanted to invite. Because when they arrived at the fishmonger's shop, there was a strangely gloomy air about the place. No one was uttering a word. Mr Petrusca himself was nowhere to be seen. Mrs Petrusca was filleting a fish in the sink behind the counter. One of her assistants was quietly giving change to a customer.

'Is Mr Petrusca in the back?' said Hazel.

Mrs Petrusca looked around. She nodded.

'Can I go through? I've brought Marcus with me to see the lobsters.'

'Hello,' said Marcus.

'I don't think Mr Petrusca will want . . . well, why not?' said Mrs Petrusca. 'Maybe it will cheer him up.'

'Cheer him up?' said Hazel. 'Is something wrong?'

'Go on, Hazel. Take Marcus with you. But if Mr Petrusca doesn't feel like talking, don't be upset.'

Hazel frowned. She began to walk slowly towards the back of the shop. The assistants were watching her. With every step she took, she felt less and less like going on.

Marcus followed her reluctantly. Suddenly, this didn't seem like a good idea at all.

It was dark in the back. At first Hazel couldn't find Mr Petrusca in the gloom. Then she spotted him, sitting on a stool in a corner with his back resting against the steel door of the freezer.

'Mr Petrusca . . .'

Mr Petrusca didn't answer.

Hazel took a couple of steps nearer. Marcus stayed in the doorway.

'Mr Petrusca, I've brought Marcus with me to see the lobsters.'

Mr Petrusca's soft blue eyes didn't flicker. They gazed vacantly past Hazel, at the other side of the room, at the tank with his two prize lobsters.

Hazel looked around.

The tank was empty.

3

THE LOBSTERS FOR Mr Trimbel had been stolen. What other explanation was there? Soon, everybody knew about it. Mr Petrusca was so unhappy that there was a whole week when he didn't come to the shop. When people asked where he was, Mrs Petrusca said he was in bed. Was he sick? No. Was he overtired? No. Was he having a holiday? No. What *was* he doing? Mrs Petrusca shrugged. She had to keep the shop going all by herself and didn't have time for long conversations. Every morning he woke up, groaned, and stayed exactly where he was, staring at the ceiling. When she came home in the evening he was still there, and it was possible he hadn't moved all day.

Finally Mr Petrusca reappeared. But he moved heavily, talked slowly and sometimes didn't seem to be listening to what people were saying. By the time they had finished telling him which fish they wanted, he had forgotten the ones they had mentioned in the beginning. It took him five minutes to fillet a trout—in the old days, it would have taken him fifteen seconds. Then he would sit down on a chair in a corner behind the counter, as if he had to recover after so much effort. Mrs Petrusca and the two assistants had to work doubly hard to make up for him. People began to say the fish wasn't filleted properly. Others complained that the quality was going down. Mr Petrusca no longer went to the fish market behind the docks every morning to pick the best and freshest of the day's catch. The assistants took it in turns. Mr Petrusca couldn't drag himself out of bed early enough.

On the day that Mr Trimbel came in to collect his lobsters, Mr Petrusca hid himself in the back of the shop. He couldn't bear to see the look of disappointment on Mr Trimbel's face. The two prize lobsters had been stolen. Mr Trimbel could understand that. But if they had been stolen, why hadn't Mr Petrusca made some effort, any effort, to replace them with ones that were at least a little bit special? The fishmonger's assistant merely fished two ordinary lobsters out of the tank in front of Mr Trimbel's eyes. That was something Mr Trimbel *didn't* understand.

No one understood. Mr Petrusca hid himself in the back of the shop more and more, and it seemed that soon he might even take to his bed again.

There was a lot of talk about Mr Petrusca amongst the Moodey children as they walked the three blocks to and from school each day. In the mornings, just about everything that happened in the Moodey Building was likely to be discussed by them. And in the afternoons, on the way home, they talked about everything again,

27

because they had all had the whole day to think about things and change their opinions.

'He's cracked!'

That was Leon Davis's opinion. They were on their way home after school, and they weren't far from the Moodey Building when Leon Davis decided it was time to discuss Mr Petrusca again. Leon was good at football and lots of people listened to him, almost as many as listened to Hazel Green.

'He's cracked, he's cracked, Petrusca's cracked!' shouted Robert Fischer, who listened to Leon Davis more than anyone else.

Robert jumped around the pavement as he chanted, and his satchel bobbed around on his back. Sometimes, if he jumped enough, it bobbed all the way up and hit him in the head.

'He's cracked, he's crack—*Ow!*' cried Robert as it hit him.

'*You're* cracked now!' shouted Marcus Bunn. Robert Fischer turned around and made a face.

'I'm telling you, he really is cracked,' said Leon Davis, looking around at the others. 'My mother says he's no good for anything any more.'

'Really?' said Maurice Tobbler, and he scratched his head as he walked, thinking.

'Yes, really, Cobbler,' said Leon Davis.

Maurice was always called Cobbler, because it rhymed

with Tobbler, and because he always took such a long time to consider everything.

'Good for nothing . . . nothing at all?' murmured Cobbler, frowning in thought.

'Yes, Cobbler!' shouted Leon Davis, and just about everyone else shouted it as well, because that was the only way to stop him asking questions that everyone else had already answered.

'That's rubbish!' said Hazel Green.

She hadn't said anything until now, because she knew Leon was only repeating what his mother had told him. That's what he did most of the time. If it wasn't his mother's opinions, it was his father's, or his football coach's. Very little ever seemed to come from Leon himself. But now everyone was looking at him, and nodding, as if it were true. And it wasn't. Besides, to say someone was good for *nothing* was an awful thing. It was such an awful thing that, if you heard it from someone else, you ought to think about it yourself before repeating it.

'It's rubbish, Leon! I've never heard you say anything stupider—and that's really saying something!'

'Oh, really?'

'Yes, really!' said Hazel. 'Good for nothing? Is that what you said?'

'Exactly!'

'Well, your mother still buys fish from him. So he's still

good for *that*—or hasn't she told you?'

Everyone laughed. Leon didn't know what to say. He stopped and faced Hazel with an angry look. Hazel gazed back just as angrily. Everyone else stopped as well, waiting to see what would happen.

Arguments between Hazel Green and Leon Davis were always exciting. *Anything* could happen, and it wasn't impossible that they would end up in a fight. Hazel and Leon each had their supporters. Who could forget the Big Brawl outside the Frengels' delicatessen? It wasn't the only brawl the Moodey children had fought, but it was the biggest, and whenever people mentioned the Big Brawl, that was the one they meant. It began after Leon complained about the girls on the football team. He was always complaining about the girls on the football team, but this time he had been doing it louder and longer than usual, so not only was he irritating, he was getting boring as well. Hazel had had enough. They happened to be outside the Frengels' delicatessen at the time, but they could have been anywhere. Hazel told him the only reason he was complaining was because the girls were better and he was frightened of losing his place on the side. This wasn't true, and Hazel knew it. Leon was the captain and the best player on team. In fact, it was such a ridiculous thing to say that Leon should have just laughed at her. But Hazel knew he wouldn't. He *hated* it when anyone refused to accept that he was a truly great player. He hated it so much that he could never see when people were just trying to upset him. It always worked. It worked that day outside the Frengels' delicatessen. In ten seconds they were wrestling. Ten seconds after that, everyone else was wrestling as well, pushing and shoving and slamming each other against the big window panes of the delicatessen, where jars of pickled cucumbers and herrings were stacked up to the ceiling.

It took half the shopkeepers in the street to pull them apart: Mr Coughlin and Mr Antoniou and Mr Petrusca and Mr Volio and Mr Butkin and Mr Frengel, and others as well. At the end they each had a pair of struggling, squirming Brawlers by the collar. It was Mr Volio who pulled Hazel and Leon apart, but she managed to get one last kick at Leon as Mr Volio dragged her away.

'Rubbish,' said Hazel once again.

Leon gazed at her, his eyes narrowed. Behind him were Robert Fischer, Hamish Rae, Sophie Wigg and Paul Boone. Behind her were Marcus Bunn, Mandy Furstow, Cobbler and Alli Reddick. Others stood close by, not yet having made up their minds which side to join.

'Two lobsters?' said Leon Davis. 'Who gets upset over *that*?'

'Yeah, who gets upset over *that*?' echoed Robert Fischer.

'Only someone who's *cracked*!'

'Yeah, only someone who's *cracked*!'

'Say that one more time, Leon, and I'll crack *you*.'

'Oh, Hazel,' said Leon, in a simpering voice. 'Are you upset as well? Are you missing your little lobster friends? I heard you used to go and visit them *all* the time.'

'Yeah, I heard you used—'

Robert Fischer stopped in mid-sentence. Hazel had turned one of her fierce, terrifying gazes on him. He knew what that meant. Leon Davis wasn't always there to protect him.

Hazel crossed her arms. 'I wouldn't be surprised if *you* took them, Leon.'

'Me?'

'Yes, you're just the kind of person who'd do it. I bet you did. Look at you, Leon. You even look guilty.'

'Yeah,' said Marcus Bunn, 'you even look guilty.'

'Wait until they catch you, Leon!'

'Yeah, wait until they—'

Marcus stopped. Leon turned back to Hazel.

'Who told you that?' said Leon sneeringly. 'The Yak?'

'I don't need the Yak to tell me. I can see it in your face, Leon.'

'That's because you're cracked, Hazel.'

'I told you what would happen if you said that again.'

'Remind me. I've forgotten.'

'Maybe I should remind you with—'

'Children!'

Hazel and Leon looked around. It was Mr Volio, on

32

the way to his bakery. He was smiling, and his arms were spread wide, as if he would have liked to give each and every one a hug.

'How nice to see you all talking happily together. So peaceful. What a wonderful sight.'

Hazel and Leon glanced darkly at each other. Then they both turned to Mr Volio and smiled back at him.

'Good,' said Mr Volio. 'Now you'd better all be getting home. It's late.'

'It isn't late,' said Marcus Bunn, looking at his watch.

'Marcus, it's late enough,' said Mr Volio. 'Almost *too* late.'

'Do you think so, Mr Volio?' said Cobbler, scratching his head.

'No, Cobbler!' everyone cried. 'It's too late for *that*!'

Mr Volio waited. He wasn't going anywhere until everyone left.

'Cracked,' whispered Leon, and he ran off before Hazel could reply.

The others left. Eventually only Hazel remained.

'It almost was too late,' said Hazel.

'Yes, it looked like that,' said Mr Volio. 'What was it this time, Hazel?'

'Leon said Mr Petrusca's cracked. He said he's good for nothing.'

'That's not very nice.'

'It was his *mother* who told him.'

33

Mr Volio shook his head. 'Mrs Davis is a bit . . . well, it isn't nice to gossip.'

'He isn't cracked, is he? Mr Petrusca, I mean.'

'Of course not, Hazel.'

'That's what I thought. But what *is* wrong with him?'

Mr Volio frowned. He shrugged, shaking his head, and began to walk towards his bakery.

4

'WHAT WOULD YOU like to eat, Hazel?' said Mr Volio.

Hazel frowned. When you were sitting in Mr Volio's bakery, this wasn't such a simple question. She hadn't had an Apricot Custlet for a while. But there was a whole batch of Cherry Flingers on a tray behind Mr Volio. And she could see Ginger Crunches, and Strawberry Combers, and Vanilla Slappers, and of course, Chocolate Dippers, which were so scrumptious that if you weren't careful you never ate anything else!

Mr Volio's bakery was a very difficult place. Nowhere else, thought Hazel, were there so many choices to be made.

'A Cherry Flinger, I think,' she said reluctantly. As soon as you chose one cake, you knew there were a whole lot of other wonderful ones you weren't going to taste— not that day, anyway.

Mr Volio gave Hazel a Cherry Flinger. Cherry Flingers were long and thin, like a submarine of icing-covered pastry with a filling of dark, plump cherries in almond cream. On the day that Mr Volio and Martin, the pastry chef, invented them, two of the apprentices had an argument and grabbed the first things that came to hand.

35

Before anyone could stop them, they were throwing the new invention at each other. It turned out that the shape of the pastries was perfect for flinging. You grabbed it by one end, and sent it spinning through the air at your opponent. By the time Mr Volio and Andrew McAndrew, the dough kneader, had separated them, the apprentices had destroyed almost the whole batch. The walls were covered with flung cream and cherries and bits of icing-covered pastry. So were the apprentices' faces! But Mr Volio wasn't at all unhappy. He didn't even make the apprentices eat a dozen éclairs, which was his usual punishment. In fact, he grabbed the last remaining Flinger and ate it with gusto. *Naming* a new pastry was always the hardest thing of all, but his apprentices had solved the problem for him, without even thinking about it!

There was no one in the bakery but Hazel and Mr Volio. Soon Mr Volio would start the furnace, and the great brick walls of his baking oven would begin to gather heat. Later the others would arrive, Andrew McAndrew, who kneaded the dough, and Martin, the pastry chef, and the four apprentices, who whipped the cream and oiled the trays and washed the tins and did all the other things that an apprentice has to do when learning to be a baker, and finally the two Mrs Volios— old Mrs Volio, who was Mr Volio's mother, and young Mrs Volio, his wife—who made the quiches and pies.

Then they would work and bake all night and be finished before everyone else got up in the morning.

But now it was quiet in the bakery. Mr Volio took some dough out of a bowl and began slapping it on the kneading table. Hazel sat beside him, eating the Cherry Flinger. The cream was so rich and thick it almost stopped your tongue moving, and the cherries were so plump they flooded your mouth with juice. But Hazel wasn't really thinking about that. And Mr Volio, for his part, didn't look like he was really thinking about the dough. He kneaded and slapped it, slapped and kneaded it, kneaded and slapped it long past the time when it didn't need kneading at all.

'I don't know about Mr Petrusca,' he said suddenly, shaking his head. 'I just don't know.'

There were a lot of people who didn't know. *She* didn't know, for example. What good did it do for two people to talk when *neither* of them knew? They'd probably just end up knowing less than they did when they began!

'Two lobsters, Mr Volio. And he wasn't even going to eat them himself!'

Mr Volio nodded, slapping the dough down for the fiftieth time and kneading it with the balls of his hands. 'Do you remember when they stole the recipe for my Chocolate Dipper last year?'

Did she *remember*? How could she forget? Mr Volio had blamed *her*. It was Harold, one of his apprentices, who had done it, and it was only after Hazel had proven it that Mr Volio had realised his mistake. That wasn't exactly the kind of thing you forgot in a hurry!

'I was very unhappy when that happened,' said Mr Volio.

'You were pretty angry, Mr Volio.'

'Yes, I know. I'm sorry, Hazel. I still feel bad about that. Would you like another cake?'

Hazel shook her head. She hadn't even finished the Cherry Flinger, and if she ate another she would have absolutely *no* room left for dinner.

'But do you know what the funniest thing was, Hazel? The thing that made me most unhappy was when I found out that it was Harold.'

'But you hardly even punished him! Twenty éclairs and a kilogram of dough—'

'Without sugar, Hazel.'

'Over two days. Over *two days*, Mr Volio!'

'It wasn't easy for him, Hazel. He struggled to finish the last éclair. I could see. I was watching.'

Hazel looked at Mr Volio doubtfully. Mr Volio slapped the dough on the table, kneaded and slapped it, avoiding Hazel's gaze.

'Anyway, the thing is, Hazel, that was what made me most unhappy. I felt like one of my apprentices had betrayed me.'

'One of your apprentices *had* betrayed you.'

'Yes, exactly. But the funniest thing is . . .'

Mr Volio paused. He held the dough in one hand. He ran the fingers of the other hand through his big walrus moustache. Hazel waited. This was the second *funniest* thing Mr Volio had mentioned. You couldn't have *two* funniest things. But Hazel didn't point' this out. Something about the look on Mr Volio's face made her keep quiet. He was frowning, as if he were trying to understand something—something that had never occurred to him before.

'The funniest thing,' he said eventually, raising a finger in the air and leaving a whole trail of doughy crumbs behind in his moustache, 'is that I would never have expected to feel *so* betrayed. Or that it would make me so unhappy.'

'I didn't know that, Mr Volio.'

Mr Volio shrugged. 'I tried not to show it.'

Hazel frowned. 'It would make me *angry*. When someone lets me down I want to go out and punch their nose!'

'Exactly,' said Mr Volio. He began to slap the dough again. 'But you see, it made me feel unhappy. Much more unhappy than I would ever have imagined if you'd asked me before.'

'But no one betrayed Mr Petrusca.'

'Someone did. Someone stole those lobsters.'

'But not his assistants. They wouldn't have done it.'

'No,' said Mr Volio. 'They're good people. I don't

know who would have.'

'I wouldn't be surprised if it was Leon Davis,' muttered Hazel. 'I really wouldn't.' She shook her head. 'Anyway, Mr Volio, you weren't as unhappy as Mr Petrusca. I've never *seen* anyone so unhappy.'

'No, that's true.' Mr Volio frowned. 'I don't know, Hazel. Maybe there's something we don't understand. No one really knew how unhappy I was about the Chocolate Dipper, and if they had, perhaps they wouldn't have understood. Maybe they would have thought, "It was just a recipe, what's he so upset about?" Or, "It was only one of his apprentices, they're always getting up to mischief." Maybe they wouldn't have realised how much it hurt me.' Mr Volio laughed. 'I wouldn't have realised it myself.'

Mr Volio put the dough down. He had kneaded it so much it was useless.

Suddenly Hazel stood up. 'This is ridiculous, Mr Volio! If there's something we don't understand, why doesn't someone ask?'

'Ask who?'

'Mr Petrusca, of course!'

5

Hazel peered hesitantly into the doorway of Mr Petrusca's shop. There were no customers inside. It was almost closing time. Mrs Petrusca was wiping down the filleting boards next to the sink. The assistants were taking boxes of fish off the display tables and carrying them into the back. At the bottom of their tank, the ordinary lobsters were crawling over each other, snapping at the food that had just been dropped into the water.

'What do you want, Hazel?' said Mrs Petrusca, as if she didn't have any time and needed to find out quickly. That was how she was now. She spoke as if she were always in a hurry and couldn't afford to wait while people gave explanations. In the old days, she would always stop to listen to people and no one ever got away without hearing her opinions in return. People even used to say there was quite a lot of gossip in the fishmonger's shop, as if that were a bad thing. But apparently people secretly liked gossip, because now they were saying that the only thing they asked you about in the fishmonger's shop was how much fish you wanted to buy—as if that were even worse!

Hazel didn't reply. Mrs Petrusca quickly turned back to

41

her work. Hazel went and looked at the lobsters in their tank. She tapped on the glass, but the lobsters ignored her. There must have been at least twenty of them, and they were all busily scrambling to get hold of the scraps of fish that were floating around them in the water. What did they think, these lobsters? Suddenly they looked up and . . . there was their food falling towards them, as if it were raining fish scraps! But of course it couldn't be *raining* fish scraps, at least not as far as lobsters were concerned, because they lived in water anyway. They wouldn't even know what *rain* was, thought Hazel. If you went up to a lobster and said 'Do you like it when it rains?', he'd just look at *you* as if you were a bit odd, just like you would look at a lobster if he came up to you and said 'Do you like it when it . . . *durgles?*', because rain to a lobster would mean no more than *durgle* to you. Hazel smiled to herself. What a ridiculous thought, talking lobsters, and what ridiculous words they used! She knew it was a ridiculous thought, which is why she couldn't resist thinking about it some more.

Durgle, Hazel decided, was what a lobster called it when food came floating through the water towards it. What a wonderful thing it would be if it could durgle for humans as well. Just imagine, if you looked up one day and found the air was full of Mr Volio's pastries, durgling all around you. You'd only have to reach out your hand and you'd have a Chocolate Dipper or a Cherry Flinger, or whatever else happened to be floating past you at the time. Of course, if everyone wanted the *same* Chocolate Dipper, things could turn unpleasant—but as long as people were prepared to wait their turn, everything would be all right. Obviously that was something lobsters didn't understand. As she watched, they were crawling and rolling all over each other in a big snapping heap, and as the ones on top reached out with their claws for a piece of the durgle, the ones underneath knocked them over and they bumped all the way down to the bottom again. But there was enough for all of them. Why couldn't they just be patient? Why couldn't—

'Hazel, we're closing now.'

Hazel looked up. The counters were bare, the filleting boards were washed and stood drying beside the sink. One of the assistants was wiping down the last of the counters with a wet cloth.

'You didn't come for fish, did you?' said Mrs Petrusca.

Hazel shook her head. 'I thought Mr Petrusca might be here.'

'And?'

Hazel frowned. 'If he was here, I thought I might say hello.'

Mrs Petrusca laughed. It was a sharp laugh, and there wasn't anything happy about it. 'Say hello? You'll be lucky if he says hello back.' She stepped aside from the doorway to the back of the shop. 'Go on.'

Hazel walked past Mrs Petrusca. The assistants watched her. She went into the back room. Mr Petrusca was sitting on his stool in the corner next to the freezer door.

'Hello,' said Hazel.

Mr Petrusca didn't reply. His eyes barely flickered.

'All right, Hazel, we're closing up.' Mrs Petrusca was standing behind her in the doorway. She sounded as impatient as the lobsters in her tank.

'I'm just . . .' she looked around the room. Suddenly she saw another stool. She ran across to it and sat down. 'I'm just going to talk to Mr Petrusca for a while. He'll let me out.'

That sharp laugh again. 'Suit yourself. The front door's open. Mr Petrusca will lock it when he decides to leave. Won't you, John? John? *Giovanni?*'

Mr Petrusca didn't answer. His wife threw up her hands and walked out.

Hazel listened to the sounds of Mrs Petrusca and the assistants leaving. She heard their footsteps and then the slamming of a door. Then the only sound was the hum of the freezer and refrigerators, and that was so low, so even and regular that after a while you ceased to hear it.

And then there was nothing. Mr Petrusca sat in his corner. Hazel glanced at him. Nothing. She glanced at him again. Pretty soon she discovered she could stare right at him, minute after minute, and he didn't seem to mind. He might as well have been a Petrusca-statue as a Petrusca-person. This was quite interesting! Usually, when you stared at someone they looked right back at you or asked what you thought you were doing or told you to go away. It was an exceptionally rare thing to be able to look at another person like that, and study their face, examine every curve and wrinkle of their skin. Of course, Hazel *had* crept in and looked at her parents when they were asleep, but you couldn't really enjoy that, because you were always worried that at any moment they might wake up and find you there. . .

A flicker! She was sure she had just seen a flicker of Mr Petrusca's eyes. Where there was one flicker, there was sure to be another just waiting to happen. And if Hazel Green couldn't make it appear, no one could.

Hazel fixed Mr Petrusca with her most penetrating gaze, which she used only in the most extreme circumstances. It almost hurt to gaze like that—she hardly dared imagine what it must be like to be on the receiving end.

There! Another flicker. She gazed even harder, screwing up her eyes, bunching up her cheeks, squishing up her nose. It really did hurt.

Mr Petrusca's head turned. Now he was looking at her. What was this girl doing sitting in his shop with her face all squashed up?

Hazel relaxed. She sighed with relief. 'Mr Petrusca, I think my eyes were just about to start spinning on their stalks.'

Mr Petrusca didn't reply.

'I've been sitting here for quite a while, you know, but you didn't seem to want any conversation. Don't worry. I was having a small conversation with myself.'

Still Mr Petrusca didn't reply. But his eyebrows rose just a fraction, as if the sight of a girl with a squashed-up face sitting in his fish shop and having a conversation with herself, even a small conversation with herself, was not something he saw every day.

'I often have conversations with myself, Mr Petrusca. To be honest,' Hazel whispered, because it *was* a kind of secret, even if there was no one else who could possibly hear them, 'I don't know anyone else who says such ridiculous things, so if I want to hear them, I have to say them myself. I like ridiculous things, Mr Petrusca. If there weren't any ridiculous things in the world, I think I'd have to invent some!'

Mr Petrusca frowned.

'Yes,' said Hazel, 'I don't understand it either. Only just now, when I was outside in your shop, and I was watching it durgle in the lobster tank, I suddenly had the most ridiculous thought: what if Mr Volio's Chocolate Dippers started durgling one day? I mean, it would be very nice, of course, but people would start fighting, just like the lobsters. Who could tell when it would durgle again? Perhaps never. I'm sure they'd fight. And that *would* be ridiculous, wouldn't it? Because it would be such a wonderful thing if it durgled Chocolate Dippers, and yet, instead of appreciating how lucky they were, everyone would start fighting over them.' Hazel shook her head. 'Ridiculous!'

All this time Mr Petrusca's frown had been getting deeper and deeper. Then he opened his mouth and spoke. 'Durgle, Hazel? What does that mean?'

Hazel laughed. 'You know what it means, Mr Petrusca. You're the biggest durgle-maker ever!'

Mr Petrusca shook his head, but Hazel only laughed even louder. 'Mr Petrusca,' said Hazel, as if she were talking to a naughty child who just wouldn't stop pretending, 'durgling is when it rains food . . . in a lobster tank. Or in any other tank, I suppose. Now, don't tell me you've never made it durgle.'

'Hazel . . .'

'Of course you have. I've seen you. And remember those two big lobsters that disappeared. In their tank it didn't just durgle fish, it durgled sea urchin and squid and clam and I don't know what else!'

Mr Petrusca was silent again. At the mention of the lobsters, his face had gone blank. Once more he stared at the empty tank where the two mighty lobsters had lived.

But Hazel was in no mood to go back to staring at Mr

Petrusca. If people found themselves together, they might as well talk. You could stare all by yourself.

She got up and stood right in front of Mr Petrusca's eyes. When he turned and looked somewhere else, she moved and stood in his way again. And again . . . and again . . . until finally Mr Petrusca looked up at her and said: 'What?'

'What's wrong with you, Mr Petrusca?'

'Nothing's wrong, Hazel.'

'Yes, there is. You're not the Mr Petrusca I knew. You could gut, slice and fillet a whole salmon in twenty seconds. I used to watch you and think you had the fastest, surest hands in the whole world. And now it takes you ten minutes, even longer than it would take me!'

Mr Petrusca looked down at his thick, red hands, spreading the fingers out, as if looking for the answer to Hazel's questions in the gaps between them.

'And you don't talk, and you don't smile, and you don't laugh, and people say sometimes you don't even get out of bed!' Hazel couldn't stop herself. Suddenly she was angry, because the old Mr Petrusca was gone, he had disappeared, and she wanted him back. 'What's happening to you, Mr Petrusca? What is it? It was only a couple of lobsters. They couldn't have been *that* important!'

Mr Petrusca was shaking his head. Still he didn't say a word.

There were tears in his eyes.

'Mr Petrusca, what is it? What is it?' Suddenly Hazel knelt next to the fishmonger. She seized his big red hands in her own. She could feel tears in her own eyes and she fought and fought to keep them back.

'You don't understand,' Mr Petrusca murmured. 'No one understands.'

'That's what Mr Volio said.'

'I'm ashamed,' he muttered, his voice choked. Now the tears really flowed and he couldn't stop them.

Suddenly Hazel jumped up. 'Ashamed?' That really was ridiculous, more ridiculous than anything Hazel had ever made up. 'Ashamed of what? It's not your fault if something gets stolen from you.' She stopped. 'No, it's not that, is it? It's not the lobsters. There's something else. There must be. Did someone betray you? Is that what makes you feel ashamed?'

Mr Petrusca shook his head.

'Then what? Who took them? What did the police say?'

Mr Petrusca took a deep breath. He wiped his tears away with the sleeve of his fishmonger's coat. 'I didn't go to the police.'

'Why not?'

'What would they have done? There were no clues . . . it was just a couple of lobsters . . . They would have laughed.'

49

Hazel didn't believe that, not for a second. 'Mr Petrusca . . .'

Mr Petrusca looked up at Hazel. He hesitated, as if he couldn't quite bring himself to speak. Then suddenly he sighed. He threw up his hands.

'There was a note, Hazel.'

'A note? And you haven't shown it to the police?'

'I haven't shown it to anyone . . . No one else even knows that it exists.'

6

'HE FOUND IT stuck to the tank the morning the lobsters were stolen,' Hazel said to Mrs Gluck. 'He'd just finished unloading his fish, and then he went to the Vienna Café, like he always does, to have a hot roll and coffee—of course they're not really open that early, they're just getting ready, but apparently they always let Mr Petrusca in—and he left the door of his shop open—apparently he always leaves it open, Mrs Gluck, which doesn't sound very wise to me—and when he came back the lobsters were gone! And in their place was a note, stuck to the side of the tank.'

'I haven't heard about a note before.'

'Exactly!' said Hazel. 'No one has.'

Hazel picked up a carnation from the pile of flowers on Mrs Gluck's work table and handed it to her. The Silversmiths Association was having its annual dinner, and its members wanted arrangements of white carnations and mauve tulips for every table, because white and mauve were their colours. There were already fourteen arrangements set out on the floor around the worktable, and there were six more to go. But the van from the Association wasn't due for another hour, so

51

there was plenty of time—plenty of time for Mrs Gluck, that is, who could put together a complicated arrangement quicker than most people could tie a posy.

'He hasn't told anyone, Mrs Gluck. He wanted me to promise I wouldn't tell anyone either.'

Mrs Gluck glanced up. 'Hazel, did you promise?'

'Of course I didn't promise ... Well, I did promise, but I promised I'd *try* not to tell anyone, because I suspected that it would be very difficult not to tell anyone, not even *one* person. And I did try.'

'And when did Mr Petrusca tell you all this?'

'Yesterday.'

Mrs Gluck chuckled, turning back to the flowers in front of her. 'You didn't try very long, did you?'

'Mrs Gluck, if it's obvious you can't do something, there's no point pretending, is there?'

'No,' said Mrs Gluck, who didn't believe in pretending either.

'And I'm only telling *you*. I'm not going to tell anyone else,' said Hazel, passing her a mauve tulip. 'He hasn't shown it to *anyone*, Mrs Gluck, not even the police.'

'Why not?'

'He said he was ashamed.'

'Ashamed?'

Hazel nodded. 'I don't know why. He wouldn't say.'

Mrs Gluck worked briskly. Her hands flew, and the arrangement took shape. Onto a round wire base she threaded carnations, tulips and sprays of leaves, and within a few minutes there was a perfect, circular bouquet with mauve and white blooms nestling in the middle. But all the time, Hazel could see, Mrs Gluck was thinking.

'What did he say was in the note, Hazel?' she asked eventually, placing the finished arrangement on the ground and picking up another wire base.

'He didn't *say*. He showed it to me.'

'He showed it to you?'

'No wonder he was confused, Mrs Gluck. I couldn't understand a word of it either.'

Now Mrs Gluck put everything down and gazed at Hazel with a very puzzled expression. 'Hazel, what do you mean?'

'Neither of us could understand it. It had "Mr Trimbel" written on the front, but when you looked inside, there were just lines and lines of words that didn't make any sense. Words I hadn't even heard of before, as if someone had made them up. I still don't see why Mr Petrusca was so ashamed. *No one* could have understood it!'

'This is very curious,' said Mrs Gluck.

Hazel nodded. 'Extremely curious.'

Mrs Gluck shook her head thoughtfully. 'Something's fishy, Hazel Green.'

Mrs Gluck began to work again.

Hazel passed her one flower after another.

Eventually, Mrs Gluck said: 'Hazel, did Mr Petrusca know who the note was addressed to?'

'Of course he knew. It was written right there on the front: Mr Trimbel. How could he *not* have known?'

'Hazel, I didn't ask if he could *not* have known. I asked if he *did* know. Not being able not to know isn't the same as knowing.'

Hazel thought about that. It was quite confusing. Not being able not to know . . .? Wasn't that the same as being able to know? And being able to know . . . Wasn't that the same as knowing?

No. Mrs Gluck was right. It wasn't! Not necessarily.

Hazel frowned. 'It's a good question, Mrs Gluck. But why wouldn't he know? It was written right there on the front. *No one* could have missed it. Now that you mention it . . . I wonder why he hadn't given it to Mr Trimbel in the first place.'

Mrs Gluck didn't reply. Hazel waited, but Mrs Gluck went on making the arrangement, and when she had finished that one she began the next. To be a florist you had to have wrists and fingers that were tireless, that could twist and twine and bundle for hours on end.

'I don't understand this,' said Hazel eventually. Mrs Gluck was right, something *was* fishy. In fact, there were quite a lot of things that didn't seem to make sense. 'Why would anyone bother writing a note that no one can understand?'

'Who says no one can understand it?' said Mrs Gluck.

'Mrs Gluck, you should have seen it. It was complete rubbish.'

Mrs Gluck shrugged. 'Maybe. Or maybe not.'

'It was, I saw it.'

'Maybe it was another language.'

Hazel shook her head. 'I don't think so. You could barely pronounce it. I can't imagine any language like that. If *anyone* understands it, it's only the person who wrote it. It was like something that someone had just . . . made up for themselves.'

'I wouldn't be so sure, Hazel. Other languages sometimes look impossible if you don't know how to speak them. I once had a customer from Peru who told me about the languages they speak in the Andes, and when he pronounced the words, I thought . . . Hazel? What are you doing?'

Hazel had jumped up from the table. 'Sorry, Mrs Gluck, I've got to go. I've just had an idea!'

Hazel ran along the pavement. She didn't stop until she came to Mr Petrusca's shop.

The fishmonger was coming out of the back, carrying a box of crabs. He had barely managed to put it down on the counter before Hazel was tugging on his sleeve.

'I've got to talk to you, Mr Petrusca.'

'Hazel, I'm busy—'

'Now, Mr Petrusca. It's important.'

'Just wait, Hazel. A moment.'

Hazel waited impatiently while Mr Petrusca picked half a dozen crabs out of the box and served the customer. As soon as he had finished, Hazel was pulling on his sleeve again.

'All right. All right, Hazel,' said Mr Petrusca, as Hazel dragged him into the back of the shop.

'Mr Petrusca, I've got to see the note again.'

'Listen, Hazel, don't you worry about that note any more. Just talking about it has made me feel better. I should have said something long ago. See? I got right out of bed this morning and I've been serving customers for almost the whole day. Let's forget about it. Let's just pretend—'

But Hazel wasn't in the mood to forget anything. 'Mr Petrusca, don't you see? The note . . . it's a code!'

7

'A CODE?' SAID Mr Petrusca.

Hazel nodded excitedly. 'That's why we couldn't understand it. We just need someone to decipher it.'

Mr Petrusca shook his head. 'Hazel, I don't want to think about that note any more.'

'Of course you do. Of course you want to think about it! What will Mr Trimbel say when you give it to him?'

'Mr Trimbel?'

'Where is it? Is it still in the desk?'

'Keep your voice down, Hazel. Do you want everyone to know?'

'Where is it, Mr Petrusca?'

'All right. Shhhhh. Just be quiet.' Mr Petrusca unlocked the desk drawer and took the note out.

Hazel seized it eagerly. She unfolded it and ran her eyes over the lines. She was right, she knew it. *Jen xluvxv cuivw su'yo spicuz ein koju,'* she said, reading the first line out. 'What does it mean, Mr Petrusca, if it isn't a code?' Mr Petrusca, who was looking over her shoulder, shrugged.

'See? Just wait until we decipher it!'

'No, Hazel,' said Mr Petrusca, holding his hand out for

the note. 'It's not that important.'

'It *is* important. It's the only clue we've got. We can't just forget about it. Besides, I know who can tell us what it means.'

'Hazel, don't you tell anyone about it. You promised you wouldn't.'

Hazel didn't think this the time to remind Mr Petrusca that she only promised she'd *try* not to tell anyone. Besides, people always remembered things differently, and who was to prove whether Mr Petrusca's memory or hers was correct?

'But I can get it deciphered, Mr Petrusca.'

'I don't want it deciphered. I just want to forget about it. Next year I'll get Mr Trimbel an even bigger pair of lobsters and I'll guard them night and day, I'll even sleep here if I have to, I'll even sleep on top of the tank if necessary—'

Sleeping on top of the tank didn't sound like a good idea to Hazel, when two hungry lobsters with sharp snappers were just waiting for you to roll over by mistake and fall in and durgle down to them. But she didn't point this out to Mr Petrusca, and she didn't hear what else Mr Petrusca might do in order to guard next year's lobsters, because before he had finished she had skipped away out of the back room, through the shop and out into the street, clutching the note in her hand.

*

Hazel tore along the pavement, threading her way between the people coming in and out of the shops, past the Frengels' delicatessen, the Coughlins' fruit shop, Mr Antoniou's tailor shop, Mrs Steene's art supply store, the Butkins' mirror shop, then weaving through the tables outside the Vienna Café as she turned the corner towards the entrance of the Moodey Building, and ran straight into . . . Marcus Bunn.

Marcus bounced off her, knocked into a lady who was walking the other way, and bounced back into Hazel again, ending up exactly where he had started.

He blinked, as if he were trying to work out whether he really had been flying around like a ping-pong ball, or whether he had just imagined the whole thing.

'You should look where you're going, Marcus,' said Hazel.

'Yes,' said the lady, and she walked off with her nose in the air.

'I've been looking for you everywhere,' said Marcus, straightening his spectacles.

'Nonsense,' said Hazel, 'if you'd looked everywhere you would have found me.'

'Leon Davis is telling everyone you're as cracked as Mr Petrusca. He's saying he would have taught you a *real* lesson except Mr Volio stopped him and anyway there's no point trying to teach *anything* to someone who's as cracked as you are.'

'Good,' said Hazel impatiently. She didn't have time for Leon Davis right now. She could deal with *him* later.

'Good? What do you mean, *good*? I can tell you where he is, if you like. And Cobbler's ready to come with us.'

'Marcus, I'm busy.'

Marcus looked all around, as if Hazel's busyness was supposed to be out there on the pavement with her. 'What are you busy with? What's that you're holding?'

Hazel looked down. It was the note.

'I've got to go,' she said.

'Where?'

'Can't say.'

'You're not going to see the Yak, are you?'

'Maybe,' said Hazel.

'Tell me! Yes or no?'

'Yes or no,' said Hazel.

Marcus glared at her angrily. His face went red. Marcus was jealous of the Yak, because Hazel sometimes preferred to visit him rather than do things with Marcus himself. If you wanted to get him angry, all you had to do was say you were going to the Yak's apartment.

'Don't worry,' said Hazel, 'I'll give him your regards.'

'Don't you dare give him any regards from *me*.'

Hazel grinned. 'Watch where you're going next time, Marcus,' she said, 'or you never know *who* you might bump into.'

Marcus didn't reply. He watched Hazel walk away.

Hazel glanced at the note in her hand. It was a code. It had to be. And if it was a code, only one person could tell her what it meant.

8

Who was the Yak? Where had he come from? Where was he going? No one knew. His name was Yakov Plonsk and he had a pointy face with a sharp chin. He and his parents had arrived a couple of years earlier and taken the apartment on the third floor where old Mr Nevver used to live. And there he stayed, coming out each day to walk to school by himself and walking home by himself as well, and hardly talking to anyone in the meantime. And no one knew what went on in his mind . . . no one except Hazel Green.

Not that Hazel knew *everything* that went on in the Yak's mind. For a start, you can't know everything that goes on in anyone's mind, and for a finish, the Yak had a particularly big and clever mind, and he wasn't likely to let anyone know all the things that jiggled around inside it. But she knew that he was a mathematician and when he was inside after school he was often working on complicated problems and very long formulas, including Fermat's Last Theorem, which, according to the Yak, was the greatest puzzle in mathematics. He also played the violin, because music, like mathematics, has order. Order. If there was one word to summarise what went on in the

Yak's mind, it was order. And if there was one word to summarise what went on in Hazel's mind, it was disorder. Or better yet, *chaos!*

Perhaps it was surprising that a boy who liked order and a girl who liked chaos should have become friends, particularly when you consider that it was Hazel herself who had first thought of Yak as a name for Yakov, and it wasn't necessarily the nicest name you could invent for a person, considering that yaks are hairy Tibetan beasts with lots of fleas. But the name wasn't really her fault, it was more a *coincidence*. It just jumped straight out of her mouth as soon as she heard about the new boy in the building, before she had ever got to know him, and suddenly everybody was using it. They had become friends by coincidence as well, when Hazel was accused of stealing the recipe for Mr Volio's Chocolate Dippers. Only the Yak believed she was innocent and was prepared to help her. Yet Hazel never once stopped to think about how strange all of these coincidences were, because a person who likes chaos doesn't stop to think about every *Why?* and *Wherefore?*, although a person who likes order will add a *When?* and a *Whether?* as well.

Being a friend with the Yak wasn't like being friendly with other people. With her other friends, Hazel did things like going to the cinema, or swimming, or playing long games of volleyball at the beach in summer, or going to Victor Square, where artists and caricaturists set up their easels and tried to get people to pay for funny pictures of themselves. But with the Yak it was a battle even to get him to think about going outside. They always ended up sitting together in the front room of his apartment and . . . talking.

Yet Hazel would always go back, and if she hadn't visited the Yak for a few days, or even a couple of weeks, which sometimes happened, she would suddenly start to feel that it was time to drop in on him again, and she would take the elevator to the third floor, and knock on the door to his apartment, and his mother would answer, and there would be the Yak, at home as usual, and then they would . . . talk. What about? Hazel herself would have found it hard to tell you exactly. For example, the Yak might tell her about some mathematical problem he was struggling with—he was always fighting great battles with difficult mathematical problems that Hazel didn't understand even when he had tried to make them as simple as he could, so simple that eventually he would throw up his hands and say they weren't even the same problems any more. And Hazel, for example, might tell him about some problem she had heard about in the Moodey Building—people were always fighting great battles with knotty difficulties in their lives and the Yak could never understand why they couldn't come up with a solution even after Hazel had explained all the other complications and considerations they had to take into account.

'It just isn't logical,' he would say with a frown. 'If they just looked at it logically, they would simply . . .'

But that was exactly the *point*. People didn't always look at things logically, and no matter how many times the Yak sat and listened to Hazel tell him about one of these situations, it always fascinated him to hear about people who didn't.

The Yak's mother opened the door. She was slim and tall and was always dressed in elegant clothes. Her hair, which swirled around and behind and above her head like a seashell, made her look even taller. The Yak's mother was unlike any other mother Hazel knew. Today she was wearing a silk gown the colour of mustard, and her fingernails were painted the colour of mustard as well. Her shoes were orange. Her hair, was brown, with streaks of gold running through it. She was holding a necklace of amber beads in one hand, as if she had just been about to put it on when Hazel knocked.

'Would you like to see Yakov?' said the Yak's mother.

'Yes,' said Hazel. Why else would she have knocked?

The Yak's mother nodded. But she didn't move to get the Yak straight away. She held the necklace up to the light, and looked up to examine it. After a moment she said to Hazel, 'What do you think of this necklace? Too much amber?'

Hazel frowned. Too much amber for what?

'I was wondering that myself,' murmured the Yak's mother. Then she turned. 'I'll bring him into the front room,' she said, as she went to get the Yak.

The Yak's apartment had furniture everywhere. In the hallway alone there was a lamp, a table, a coat stand, a small desk, a set of bookshelves, two chairs, a shoe rack, a porcelain vase, a potted plant, a magazine holder, a grandfather clock, an enormous urn for umbrellas and a pair of silver candlesticks, not to mention the oil paintings on the walls and the Persian rug on the floor. The front room was full of sofas and armchairs. Hazel had been there so often that she knew which ones were comfortable and which had springs that poked up on one side and collapsed on the other. She sat down on a plump blue armchair and waited. The Yak arrived a few minutes later.

'Hello,' said the Yak, who always started things off very formally.

'I hope I haven't disturbed you.' Hazel said that only because the Yak seemed to expect it. Since he was always thinking about something or other, it was impossible *not* to disturb him.

The Yak didn't reply. He sat down.

'Were you working on a mathematical problem?' said Hazel.

'I was playing the violin . . .'

That was odd. Hazel hadn't heard any music while she was waiting.

'. . . in my head.'

'In your head!' Hazel grinned.

The Yak tried not to smile. 'You *can* play in your head, you know,' he said, trying to be serious.

'I bet you don't make as many mistakes!' said Hazel, laughing.

Now the Yak couldn't help grinning as well. That was one of his weaknesses; he always grinned when something was funny, even when he didn't want to.

'I bet the neighbours don't complain as much!'

The Yak laughed. His whole pointy face screwed up. That was another one of his weaknesses, the way his face scrunched up when he laughed.

'Wait a minute—how can you tell when someone else is playing in their head?' said Hazel.

'You can't,' said the Yak.

'So you could just be sitting there, and I could be talking, and all the time you could be playing your violin in your head?'

The Yak didn't reply. His face had taken on a serious, composed look.

'Yakov!'

The Yak grinned.

Hazel looked at him suspiciously. 'Now, listen, Yakov, you've got to concentrate. I've got a problem for you.'

The Yak sat forward eagerly in his chair.

'What is it?' he said. 'Is Mr Nimsky still complaining because his wife won't let him sell the farm he inherited from his great-uncle the Polish captain? If only they'd be logical about it, they'd see that all they have to do—'

'They sold the farm,' said Hazel.

'See. I told you—'

'To Mrs Nimsky's cousin.'

'Mrs Nimsky's cousin?' The Yak frowned.

No one liked Mrs Nimsky's cousin—except Mrs Nimsky's aunt, of course—because he gambled too much and had once borrowed Mrs Nimsky's car for an evening and had come back the next morning without it. The car hadn't been stolen. Mrs Nimsky's cousin knew exactly where it was—because after he had lost it in a card game he had driven it himself to the house of its new owner!

'Yes,' said the Yak, 'that is a problem.'

'No, it's not—well, it is, now that you mention it,' said Hazel, 'but that's not the problem I'm talking about. This problem is something you'll find much more interesting.'

Hazel took the note out of her pocket and handed it to the Yak. The Yak glanced at it, and handed it back to Hazel.

'Read it.'

'Why?'

'Go on, just read it.'

Hazel shrugged. She began to read.

'Jen xluvxv cuivw su'yo spicuz ein koju,
A ohzovw pawu (kex xc o slapnun).
Ax'p gpoov qe qo xlo ero xe xpoju—
Xlo Japlqir eb Vukezk, Suqvipgo!

Wuivgd lacl okh paz, ak oph xlo wlasw—
Glogn oyunc xirn, pajq uyovc xoxyl.
Cee qaclx iw zopp xu fecakk gdesp
Ow qvc qe foox Luxniwyo'w yoxyl!

We bev i glirko, mipx ekgu i zakrun,
A xdeiclx ux zaipz fu kago xe xu.
Aj vei pxahp zirx aiv hefpxun hakrun—
Cee'pp barz ax soaqarc lunu zuxl ju!'

By the time she was finished the Yak had collapsed in his chair, his face was scrunched, his legs were kicking, and his sides were splitting with laughter.

'What's so funny?' demanded Hazel. 'What does it mean?'

The Yak shrugged, gasping. 'I don't know. You sounded so ridiculous . . . I just had to hear you read it.'

Hazel folded her arms and fixed the Yak with an especially stern look. The Yak stopped laughing. He sat up in his chair. Hazel waited until he was serious again. Then she handed him the page.

'It's code, of course,' said the Yak, after looking at it

for a moment.

'I knew it! I knew it was a code.'

'Where did you get it?' said the Yak, still studying the words.

'I'll tell you later. First—can you decipher it?'

'Probably.' The Yak gazed at the page. 'The vowels and consonants are treated separately. You can see that immediately.'

'Can you? How?'

The Yak didn't answer. Hazel could see his eyes flicking over the lines. Suddenly he nodded his head, then his eyes searched the page some more.

'Look, you see that word there,' he said, holding out the paper and pointing to the second line, 'that says "got". You see, k . . e . . x—g . . o . . t. Each letter is going forward three. Vowels and consonants separately. And this word . . . No, that's not right,' The Yak was frowning. 'Wait a minute . . . That wasn't "got" at all. It's something else . . . This is getting more interesting.'

Suddenly the Yak stood up.

'Where are you going?'

The Yak didn't answer. He went out and came back a minute later with a pen and paper. He put the paper down on the coffee table in front of him. He laid the note out flat next to it. He took off his watch and laid it down as well. He wrote the alphabet across the top of the page. And now, with a glance at his watch, he really began to work.

Under the Yak's pen, the paper filled with letters and words. He scribbled across the page, crossed things out, and scribbled again. He put his pen to his lips, thought, and wrote some more. The minutes passed. After a while he turned to a fresh page, wrote the alphabet at the top, and began scribbling all over again.

Hazel watched. She hoped he'd decipher it soon— from the way he was concentrating it looked like he was capable of working for six hours straight without looking up once!

Hazel kicked her legs. She decided to stare very hard at the Yak, to see if he could keep working. He did! Nothing could upset his concentration. At one point the Yak's mother put her head round the door. Hazel grinned, cocking her head in the Yak's direction. The Yak's mother nodded and tiptoed away again.

The Yak continued to work. Suddenly he smiled. He glanced at his watch. Then he sat back and looked at Hazel.

At last! Two hours must have gone by at least.

'Forty-eight minutes,' said the Yak. 'Not bad.'

Hazel glanced at him suspiciously. 'Are you sure your watch hasn't stopped?'

'Very funny. Do you want to know the code or not?'

'Of course I want to know, Yakov. Why do you think I've been sitting here for three hours?'

'Under an hour, Hazel. Admit it!'

'I admit it. It was so much fun it just *seemed* like three hours.'

'All right, listen. The code works like this: each letter is represented by the letter three places after it in the alphabet—consonants and vowels separately, as I said at the start. But every *third* letter is represented by the letter three places *before* it. That was the tricky bit. That's why it took so long. I could see there was a shift, but I couldn't tell exactly what it was. It's really a simple shift—I was trying to work out much more complicated solutions. It just proves the old principle that you should always try the simplest ideas first. Here, see for yourself.'

The Yak handed the note to Hazel.

'Oh, and you start numbering each line separately,' he said.

Hazel handed the note straight back. The Yak was just showing off, and they both knew it.

'Yakov, just tell me what it says.'

The Yak grinned. 'Don't you want to know the code?'

'Yakov . . .'

'All right,' he said. 'I'll tell you what it says.'

The Yak turned to a clean page. He wrote the alphabet at the top again, and then, glancing back and forth between the alphabet and the note, he rapidly wrote twelve lines. When he had finished, he sat back and read them.

He looked puzzled. 'Winner? . . . Dinner? . . .' he

murmured. He handed the paper over to Hazel.

Hazel read. The Yak watched her.

'Does it make any sense to you?' he said.

Hazel didn't reply. Her eyes went wide as she read the lines.

9

IT WASN'T LEON Davis who had stolen Mr Petrusca's lobsters. Deep down, Hazel had known all along it wouldn't turn out to be him. He wouldn't have had the audacity to do it. Even though stealing lobsters was a nasty thing to do, it would have taken courage, and Leon only seemed to have any courage when he had about thirty of his friends to back him up. Besides, it took real intelligence to write a code that only someone like the Yak could solve—more intelligence than Leon Davis had, that was for sure. But she had still been hoping, somehow, that it *might* be him, and that she *might* be able to catch him with the Yak's help.

No, it wasn't Leon Davis. Hazel read the code-poem again, shaking her head in amazement. It was just about the *last* person you would have suspected.

> *'For thirty years we've played our game,*
> *I always lose (not by a whisker).*
> *It's clear to me the one to blame —*
> *The Fishman of Renown, Petrusca!*

74

Search high and low, in all the shops—
Check every tank, sift every batch.
You might as well be buying chops
As try to beat Petrusca's catch!

So for a change, just once a winner,
I thought it would be nice to be.
If you still want our lobster dinner—
You'll find it waiting here with me!'

It was clear. The code-poem left no room for doubt.
The lobsters were part of some kind of competition, and
the thief was the very person who had the special dinner
with Mr Trimbel each year—his friend!

'Well?' said the Yak, who was still watching her.

Well, thought Hazel, from here on, nothing could be
simpler. All Mr Petrusca had to do was to show Mr
Trimbel the note and the translation. Then it was up to
Mr Trimbel himself. He ought to make his friend go to
Mr Petrusca and apologise and pay for the lobsters . . . No,
but that wasn't enough. He ought to come to the shop and
clean up on Saturday afternoons for three months, just to
show how sorry he was for playing such a mean trick . . .
And not even that was enough! He ought to go to the fish
market with Mr Petrusca for the next four weeks to help
carry the boxes of fish in and out of the van. Getting up at

two o'clock in the morning for a month might teach him a lesson or two . . . And not even *that* was enough! He ought to . . .

'Hazel?'

Hazel looked up. 'That was very helpful, Yakov.'

'But what's it about?'

'Oh, it's not important.'

'Really?'

Hazel shook her head. The Yak, she knew, wouldn't bother thinking about it for long. Soon he'd be puzzling over some mathematical problem or playing the violin in his head again.

The Yak nodded. 'There's a very interesting mathematical problem I'm working on, Hazel. Shall I tell you about it?'

'Next time, Yakov. I've got to go now.'

'But I'll have solved it by next time!'

'But the solution will raise five *more* problems, and you can tell me about them instead,' said Hazel.

'All right,' said the Yak. Hazel was right. Every solution always raised more questions—that was the best thing about mathematics!

All the way back to Mr Petrusca's shop, Hazel was making up punishments for the lobster thief. In the end, she had so many she didn't know which to choose. Mr Petrusca could decide, she thought, as she turned into his shop. Anyone who spent their whole life slitting, gutting and filleting fish—not to mention cracking oysters and shelling shrimps—would be sure to have some good ideas of his own!

But not everything was as clear as Hazel imagined, and there was still *some* room for doubt even after the translation of the code-poem. Perhaps, if she had taken a bit more time to think it through, instead of hurrying straight back to Mr Petrusca from the Yak's apartment, Hazel would have realised it. There was still one small but puzzling detail which no amount of code-breaking could decipher—because it hadn't needed deciphering at all!

In fact, if Hazel hadn't been so eager to get the note from Mr Petrusca in the first place, she would have realised that it was the *first* problem she should have solved.

Why hadn't Mr Petrusca already given the note to Mr Trimbel . . . whose name was written in clear, plain English on the front?

10

'MR PETRUSCA, I'VE got it!' Hazel yelled, waving the note as she opened the door of the fish shop.

Mr Petrusca jumped. 'Shhhh!' he cried. Everyone had heard her, Mrs Petrusca, and the assistants, and three customers who were waiting for their fish.

Mr Petrusca came out from behind the counter. 'Shhhh!' he said again, although that only made everyone wonder even more what he was *shhhhing* about, and then he pushed Hazel towards the back of the shop, pushed her quite roughly, in fact, and she almost stumbled.

That wasn't what she expected. She'd just done him a big favour! But maybe Mr Petrusca didn't know his own strength. After all, he was used to shoving heavy boxes of fish around.

'What, Hazel? What have you got?'

No, that didn't sound friendly.

They were in the back of the shop. Mr Petrusca closed the door.

'The note, Mr Petrusca. I've had it deciphered.'

'Have you?' he said angrily.

'Yes, I have. I told you I would. Look!'

Hazel threw the note down triumphantly on the desk.

Then she threw the translation down next to it. She turned excitedly to Mr Petrusca.

But Mr Petrusca wasn't looking at the pages at all. He was staring at her. Then suddenly he slumped down on a stool and buried his face in his hands.

'Mr Petrusca?'

Slowly, Mr Petrusca lowered his hands and turned to look at Hazel. The anger in his eyes was gone. But there was no gratitude there either.

'What is it, Mr Petrusca?' Hazel pleaded. 'Don't you want to know what it says? It's not bad, it's nothing to be frightened of. It's not the best poem I ever read. And don't be upset, but they rhymed your name with "whisker", because they couldn't think of a real rhyme, I suppose, but it *is* hard to find a rhyme for "Petrusca". I tried to think of one myself just now and I couldn't. See, Mr Petrusca,' said Hazel, and she picked up the Yak's translation and held it out to him, 'it's nothing bad.'

Mr Petrusca took the paper out of her hand. He gazed at it for a long time. His hand dropped and rested limply against the desk, and the paper sagged over it. He stared and stared.

'Mr Petrusca?'

Mr Petrusca tossed the paper onto the table. He looked up at Hazel again. He shook his head and sighed. It was a deep sigh, as if it came from somewhere as deep as the sea from which his fish were caught.

'You don't understand, do you, Hazel?'

'I don't understand, Mr Petrusca.'

Mr Petrusca nodded. When he spoke, the words were so soft, so quiet, they were less than a whisper, just a breath of sound.

'I can't read, Hazel.'

11

'NOTHING?'

Hazel shook her head in astonishment. She sat down next to Mr Petrusca, and glanced at him out of the corner of her eye, and then shook her head again.

'That's amazing! Nothing?' she said to herself. 'No, you must be able to read *something*, Mr Petrusca.'

'Must I?' murmured Mr Petrusca.

Hazel frowned. 'Nothing? Nothing at all? But *everyone* can read! I learned to read when I was five. By the time I was eight, well, I could read just about anything, even newspapers. Not everyone learns that quickly, of course, but—'

Hazel stopped. Maybe that wasn't the right kind of thing to say. Mr Petrusca had buried his face in his hands again.

Suddenly Hazel understood.

'That's what makes you ashamed, isn't it?'

Mr Petrusca didn't reply.

'It wouldn't make *me* ashamed. It would make me want to go out and—'

Hazel stopped again. No, that wasn't right either.

'I'm sorry, Mr Petrusca. You've got to understand, it's

very surprising to hear someone say they can't read—an adult, I mean. I've heard adults say they can't ride a bike . . . or they can't swim . . . My father can't swim, for instance, but he's promised to let me teach him in the summer. But not reading? Well, that *is* unusual. I've never heard an adult say that before!'

'I'd rather not be so unusual,' murmured Mr Petrusca.

'Maybe not.' Hazel gazed at Mr Petrusca with curiosity. 'Why didn't you ever learn to read? Didn't you go to school?'

'Yes.'

'Didn't anyone teach you?'

'They tried.'

'Maybe they didn't try the right way. Take me, for example. Now, I have a teacher who tries to teach me pottery, but no matter how hard he tries, none of my pots come out smooth. They're always lumpy, or crooked, or the rims—which are meant to be perfectly round and perfectly level, Mr Petrusca—come out all wavy. I just don't understand why that happens. I listen very carefully to what he says, and I do it all as carefully as I can, and I always finish quicker than anybody—because pottery is quite boring, Mr Petrusca, and I'd rather do almost anything else, even if it's just sitting there and listening to my own thoughts while everybody else finishes, and that can take quite a while, because Abby Simpkin takes *twice* as long as me, because she thinks she's going to be a truly great potter and *ceramicist*, whatever that's supposed to mean—it's her word, because she's even better at English than pottery, and knows quite a few words that nobody else has ever heard of, at least none of us, and even the teachers admit they sometimes haven't heard of them, but I think she just looks them up in dictionaries and memorises them to impress everyone, and . . . and . . .' Hazel stopped to catch her breath, wondering why she had started talking about Abby Simpkin, or pottery, for that matter, and how she ended up where she had ended up and how she was going to connect it to what she had been saying at the beginning.

Mr Petrusca was watching her, and there was even a little smile on his face, which made Hazel feel better about having got lost in her pottery story, and made her wonder whether she had made an important discovery: that pottery, in small doses, can be quite a cheerful thing!

'Anyway,' said Hazel, 'the point is, Mr Petrusca, I'm sure my pots could be just as smooth as Abby Simpkin's. But I'm not being taught in the right way. I'm being taught in the way that's right for Abby.'

'Hazel,' said Mr Petrusca, 'do you really think that's the reason?'

'Of course it's the reason. Or it's *a* reason.' Hazel shrugged. It *could* be the reason. There were always so many possible reasons for just about anything, and who was to say which was right and which one wasn't? 'What about you, Mr Petrusca? Is that the reason you never learned to read?'

The smile disappeared from Mr Petrusca's face.

'Mr Petrusca?'

'I don't know, Hazel. I never found it very easy. And after a while, no one seemed to bother. Everyone ignored it. I went from one class to the next.'

'How?'

'I don't know.' Mr Petrusca looked at Hazel with an expression of genuine astonishment, as if he couldn't understand it either. 'It just happened. I pretended to be able to read, and . . . I suppose . . . the teachers pretended I could as well. They *must* have known. I used to guess what things said, or I'd try to remember what the other boys read out—but I was *always* making mistakes. Yet no one seemed to be bothered! Up I went, from one class to the next. And what happens when you find a great big boy of eight, or ten, or even *twelve* years, who can't read? Maybe you think, well, it's too late. Too late to teach him now. He had his chance. He was probably too stupid to learn when he was six years old, so he'll still be too stupid now.'

'You're not stupid, Mr Petrusca! You're the cleverest fishmonger I've ever met.'

Mr Petrusca shook his head. 'Of course, I couldn't pretend for ever,' he said, gazing at the tabletop in front of him. 'It had to end. So that's when I left school and went to work for Mr O'Grady, who was the fishmonger here before me. It didn't matter to him that I couldn't read—he couldn't read either.'

'Another one!' cried Hazel in amazement.

'Do you think it's so rare?' demanded Mr Petrusca suddenly. 'I could name you five other people who can't read—and you know them all!'

'Who?'

'And in your class at school, Hazel? Do you think there isn't *someone* who's like I was, trying to hide that he can't read properly? Maybe you all think he's stupid—maybe you even tell him he is, like people told me.'

Hazel was silent. There *were* some people at school . . . Sometimes people *did* call them names, told them they *were* stupid. She frowned, wondering about them. She just thought they were stupid.

Hazel looked up at Mr Petrusca. 'But how can you manage? You're not at school now. You have a business to take care of.'

'It's not as hard as you think. I've learned to recognise the names and numbers I need. There aren't that many. And I'll tell you a secret,' said Mr Petrusca, dropping his voice, 'no one else wants to know either. No one wants to know that other people can't read. *Everybody's* ashamed of it. It's not pleasant. It makes everyone embarrassed—so everyone ignores it. Just like at school—if you pretend you can read, everyone else will pretend with you.'

Hazel couldn't believe this! How could everybody pretend that something they all knew about just wasn't true? It was like the story about the emperor who went out without any clothes—he pretended he was dressed, and so did everyone else. But that was just a story—this was real life!

'Well, what about Mr Trimbel's friend?' she said suddenly. 'What are you going to do about him? Who is he, anyway?'

Mr Petrusca waved his hand. 'I don't know his name. He lives in the Greville Building, I think.' Suddenly Mr Petrusca frowned. 'Why should I do anything about Mr Trimbel's friend?'

'Because he's the one who stole the lobsters! It says so in the poem. Listen, I'll read it to you.'

Hazel picked up the Yak's translation and read it aloud.

'So,' said Mr Petrusca when she had finished, '*that's* what it was all about!'

Hazel stared at Mr Petrusca in amazement. He was shaking his head and chuckling.

'You're not going to let him get away with it!' she said.

'Hazel, listen. It was only a couple of lobsters—'

'Prize lobsters! Kings of the sea!'

'A couple of lobsters, Hazel. And besides, he says that no one can beat mine. That's a compliment. Listen, if that was the worst thing that ever happened to me because I couldn't read—someone taking a couple of lobsters—I'd be a very happy man.'

Hazel shook her head. *What was going on?* 'Mr Petrusca, if those lobsters weren't so important, why did it make you feel so bad when they were taken? You're hardly ever sad and miserable like that . . . like you were . . . Mr Petrusca, you're normally one of the happiest people I know!'

The fishmonger smiled. 'Thank you, Hazel.'

'Don't thank me, Mr Petrusca. I still don't understand.'

Mr Petrusca frowned. He thought for a couple of minutes. 'Well, I over-reacted.' Mr Petrusca paused to think again. Then he nodded to himself. 'You see, when you can't read—or when you have anything to hide, I suppose—you create a sort of . . . safety area. That's the best way I can describe it, Hazel. An area where you're safe, a routine that you know. For instance, in my shop, and when I go to the fish market, I can recognise all the words and numbers I need. And if I need to know something else when I'm there—at the fish market, for example—I can always find a way of getting someone to tell me without making them suspect. They're my friends. Everything's familiar. But if I go somewhere else, everything's strange. You never know what words you'll need to recognise, or whether you'll find anyone to tell you. And if you do find someone, you have to hope you

87

can ask in such a way that they won't suspect why you're asking. You just feel as if . . . someone's going to discover your secret at any moment.'

'So you never go outside your safety area?'

'I suppose not. Not if I can help it,' said Mr Petrusca.

Hazel frowned. Discovering new things was the best fun of all. That was what the world was *for*. She could barely imagine what it would be like to be trying *not* to discover new things all the time. What kind of a way was that to live?

'When I saw that note,' said Mr Petrusca, 'I panicked. It's as simple as that, Hazel. I knew that if I did anything with that note—told anyone about it, or went to the police—they'd ask me questions about it. They'd ask why I didn't know what was written there. I'd be outside my safety area.'

'But it was in code!' Hazel objected. 'No one could tell what was written there.'

'I didn't *know* it was in code. Hazel—I couldn't read it!' exclaimed the fishmonger in exasperation. 'Code or no code, it all looks the same to me. Don't you understand?'

Hazel nodded, slowly. She was beginning to understand.

'So ask yourself: what would have happened? They'd have asked questions. Or I'd have to fill in a form, and they'd see I couldn't write. One way or another, they'd find out. And then everyone would know. And that morning, when I found that empty tank, it all came back

88

to me . . . what it used to be like, when I was young. When you grow up, Hazel, you can make your own safety area, you can create your own routine. But when you're young, at school, it's hard. It's impossible. It all came back to me. Suddenly I felt all the old shame again. I could almost hear people crying out, "Stupid John, his reading's wrong!" like they did when I was a boy. And then I thought, "Look at yourself, Giovanni Petrusca, worried about losing your safety area. How can a grown man like you even need a safety area? Worrying that you'll get lost driving your van one day, because you won't even be able to read the street signs to work out how to get home!" And that just made me even more ashamed. What kind of a way is that to live?'

Hazel shook her head. She didn't know what to say. For a moment Mr Petrusca was silent as well. From the front of the shop they could hear the voice of a customer and the sound of water gushing into a sink.

'You see,' Mr Petrusca said eventually, 'I over-reacted. And the more I thought about it, the more ashamed I felt. It just got worse and worse. Every day I felt more unhappy. And the unhappier I felt—the unhappier I became! I'd managed to organise things so well that I'd just forgotten what it was like to be outside my safety area. That was the mistake. I should have been ready. I *always* have to be ready. It's a good lesson. It serves me right for forgetting.'

'It does *not* serve you right.'

'It does. I have to be realistic, I have to be prepared. But Hazel, I'm feeling much better about it now. It was all bottled up inside me. Talking to someone—telling *you*—has made me feel better. So I'm going to put it all behind me!' Mr Petrusca stood up, and stretched his arms, just as if he were getting out of bed for a brand-new day. 'The best thing is to forget it, pretend it didn't happen. Mr Trimbel's friend meant no harm. And no one found out, that's the main thing. No one found out, and no one has to.'

More pretending, thought Hazel. When would it end?

'What's to stop it happening again, Mr Petrusca? Why don't you learn to read? That's the only real safety area— and if you learned to read, you wouldn't even need one.'

'Learn to read? At my age? If I couldn't learn as a boy, what chance do I have now?' Mr Petrusca shook his head. 'No, Hazel. No one has to find out, right?'

Hazel looked up at Mr Petrusca. His soft blue eyes searched her face anxiously.

'No, Mr Petrusca, no one needs to find out.'

Mr Petrusca relaxed, smiling at her. 'Thank you, Hazel . . . Thank you.' He stood up and, after one last glance, went out to the front of the shop.

Hazel looked at the empty lobster tank against the wall. No, no one needed to find out. She couldn't bear the thought of the shame Mr Petrusca would feel if his secret became known.

Yet she could hardly bear the thought of letting Mr Trimbel's friend, the one who started the whole thing, get away scot-free.

How could she prevent one without allowing the other? That was the question.

Hazel looked back at the desk. The code-poem and the translation were still lying in front of her.

She folded the pages and slipped them into her pocket.

12

'STILL MISSING YOUR *lobsters*, Hazel?' Leon Davis asked with a grin as they were all walking to school a few days later.

'Yeah, still missing them?' demanded Robert Fischer, and he put up his arms and snapped his hands like a pair of claws above his head.

Hazel snapped at Robert's nose. He ran off down the street with his satchel bobbing on his back.

'I heard Mr Petrusca's much better,' said Leon. 'He isn't cracked any more. Someone must have glued him together.'

Leon Davis laughed. So did the others. Even Marcus Bunn giggled.

'I wonder who it was,' said Leon.

'He never was *cracked*,' said Hazel, 'I've told you before.'

'You seem to know so much about it. Maybe *you* glued him together.'

'Yeah, like Humpty Dumpty,' said Robert Fischer, who had bobbed back.

'You're so ridiculous, Robert,' said Hazel. 'No one could glue Humpty Dumpty together. That was the whole point.'

Robert Fischer frowned. 'Was it?'

'Of course it was,' said Hamish Rae, and he went up to Robert and began to whisper in his ear. *'Humpty Dumpty sat on a wall—Humpty Dumpty had a big . . .'*

'Well?' said Leon Davis.

'Well what?'

'What do you know about it?'

'Nothing,' said Hazel. She knew *everything* about it—but she certainly wasn't going to tell Leon Davis. She wasn't going to tell anyone.

'She went to visit the Yak,' said Marcus Bunn.

Hazel turned around and glared at him. Marcus was always her strongest supporter—except when it came to the Yak. Leon Davis crowed with delight.

'So, you went to visit the Yak. You must know something.'

'More than you, that's for sure!' said Hazel.

They were at the intersection of Fursten Avenue. They stopped while they waited for the lights to change. School was only a short distance away, you could already see its clock tower over the other buildings. People were converging on it from all directions. The children from the Burbank Building were coming down Fursten Avenue from the left. A big group from the Greville and Moray Buildings was approaching from the right.

'Hazel,' said Leon.

The lights changed. They began to cross.

'Hazel, are you coming to see the old sailing ships when they arrive?'

'Why do you care, Leon?'

'Everyone's going to be there.' Leon glanced up the street. 'The Grevillers especially.'

Hazel glanced at the Greville children. No matter how many arguments they had with each other, everyone from the Moodey Building stuck together when it came to people from other buildings. There was never any doubt about that.

'*Everyone's* going to be there, Hazel. Saturday week,' said Leon.

Marcus Bunn, and Cobbler, and the others were watching her.

'Everyone?' said Hazel.

'They're all talking about it.'

Hazel nodded, 'All right. I'll be there.'

'See, I told you, Leon,' said Marcus Bunn.

Leon nodded, but he didn't say anything else, because a moment later the Grevillers arrived from one side and the Burbankers arrived on the other, and they all merged into one big, shouting, jostling mass, as they poured through the school gate.

Yet seeing the old sailing ships when they came to the port, and milling around with all the other crowds of children that were going to be there, was the last thing on Hazel's mind.

She kept thinking about Mr Petrusca. Imagine having to live like that, always worried you would drop a clue, always frightened someone would find out. Always frightened of anything new. Did Mrs Petrusca know? Maybe Mr Petrusca pretended to her as well.

It was all very strange. Did adults really do things like that? Were there really adults who couldn't read, and who spent their time pretending that they could? It was the sort of thing that only little children were supposed to do.

But what if it were true? Imagine living your whole life like that . . . having to pretend *all* the time!

'Hazel, don't you think it's time to put that marigold down?'

Hazel looked up with a start. She frowned. She was holding a green stalk and the lumpy bit from the middle of a flower. Orange petals lay all over the table. And yet the last thing Hazel could remember was that she had just picked up a marigold to look at it!

'I'm sorry, Mrs Gluck.'

Mrs Gluck laughed. 'Picking at flowers is a sure sign of troubled thoughts. Whenever I pick at flowers, I know something's wrong.'

'Nothing's wrong.'

Mrs Gluck nodded. Her hands kept working, binding the stems of a bunch of yellow zinnias that she was setting with purple iris buds. The zinnias were as round as a baby's fist, and the iris buds were like spears that would burst open with a fountain of petals.

Mrs Gluck finished the arrangement and stood it in a vase. She sat down on a stool beside her work table. 'Time for a rest. Would you do me a favour, Hazel? Would you mind taking that bucket of chrysanthemums out to Sophie? We need some more in the front.'

Hazel picked up the bucket. The chrysanthemums were a special type, huge balls of colour, red and yellow. She took them out to Sophie, who was serving a customer.

'I was just coming to get those,' said Sophie, as soon as the customer had gone.

'Of course,' said Hazel. Sophie was always *just* coming to get something as soon as Mrs Gluck brought it out for her.

'Tell Mrs Gluck we'll be needing some more of those daffodils soon.'

'They're just inside the other room,' said Hazel.

'Thank you, Hazel,' said Sophie, in a tone that didn't sound very thankful at all.

'They're just waiting for you to come for them. You can almost hear them saying to each other, "Where's Sophie? Where is she? She promised she'd come for us."'

Sophie rolled her eyes. She went over to the display of bouquets and stood in front of them, examining them closely. Sophie spent almost all her time arranging the bouquets, which, in her opinion, was a job of great importance. She would stand in front of them, turning them one way and another, moving them a centimetre forward or a centimetre backwards on the shelf. Then she would go away to serve a customer and when she came back to them she would do exactly the opposite of what she had done before.

Sophie glanced over her shoulder and saw that Hazel was still there. She started humming to herself. She picked one of the bouquets up, turned it round, turned it round again, and put it down. Then she stood back and looked at it once more, as if to see whether the display was any better.

'Where is she? Oh, where is Sophie?' Hazel sang in a high, sad voice, before she went back to Mrs Gluck's workroom.

Mrs Gluck was peering at her order book.

'What would you do if you didn't have an order book, Mrs Gluck?' said Hazel.

Mrs Gluck looked up with a start. She hadn't realised that Hazel had returned. 'Well, I'd get one, of course. In fact, as soon as I start a new one, I buy another, so I always have one spare.'

'No,' said Hazel, sitting down beside her. 'What if you couldn't use one?'

'Couldn't use one? Why couldn't I use one?'

'Well, what if you were blind?'

'Blind? Oh, that would be a terrible thing. I don't know what I'd do. Do you think I could still make my bouquets? Perhaps I could, with assistance. Sophie would have to help, of course.'

Hazel snorted.

'I'm sure she'd help, Hazel. She's a good girl.'

'She doesn't listen to the daffodils,' muttered Hazel.

Mrs Gluck gave her a puzzled look. '*Listen* to the daffodils?'

'That's not what I meant.'

'No, you meant look after the daffodils. It's true, sometimes she—'

'No, that's not what I meant either, Mrs Gluck.'

'Hazel Green, sometimes I don't know what you mean.'

Good, thought Hazel. It was no good if people knew what you meant all the time!

'About being blind, Mrs Gluck. I didn't mean that. I meant, what would happen if you just couldn't use an order book?'

'But I still don't see why not. They're not thinking of making a law against order books, are they? They're always sending out regulations about one thing or another. Only last week the council sent all the shopkeepers a note to say the day's rubbish had to be out front by seven in the evening. I don't usually close before eight. And besides, I don't put my rubbish out the front— I put it out the back!'

'I don't think they're making a law against order books,' said Hazel. 'But what if you *still* couldn't use one. Let's say . . .' Hazel paused, and put her finger to her lips, and stared up at the ceiling for a very long time, so Mrs Gluck would realise that there were lots of possible reasons, so many that it really took a long time to choose—and just because you came out with one, it didn't mean you couldn't have come out with another. 'Let's say . . . well, you couldn't read, for instance.'

'Couldn't read?'

'No,' said Hazel, as nonchalantly as she could. 'For instance.'

Mrs Gluck gave Hazel a long, searching glance. Hazel hated it when Mrs Gluck did that. She felt as if she could see right through her.

'Well, that *is* an interesting thought,' said Mrs Gluck. She stood up and began collecting the flowers for her next arrangement. 'Any particular reason you thought of it?'

'No,' said Hazel.

'Any particular person you're thinking of?' said Mrs Gluck.

Hazel shook her head.

Mrs Gluck continued to gaze at Hazel for a moment. 'Well, let me think,' she said eventually. Mrs Gluck began separating the flowers out and laying them side by side. She had picked out orange peonies, yellow tulips and three cream-coloured rosebuds. The roses would give a wonderful coolness to the hot colours of the peonies and tulips, and she had selected a variety of dark leaves as well to give the arrangement shape and depth. 'If I couldn't read, I don't know how I'd manage. I honestly don't.'

'You couldn't, could you?' said Hazel. 'It isn't possible.'

'I didn't say I *couldn't*, Hazel. I said I didn't know how I would. It certainly is possible. People can manage all kinds of things. I had a customer once who told me he'd been lost in the Mexican desert for three weeks. Impossible, you might say. Do you know how he survived? He cut open cactuses and squeezed them for water. Would you have thought of that?'

Probably, thought Hazel. Why *shouldn't* she have thought of it?

'People can do amazing things. Do you think there aren't people out there who can't read, going about their normal business, day after day?'

'There might be one . . . or two . . .'

Mrs Gluck shook her head. She began to work on the arrangement, starting with one of the peonies in the middle. She'd leave the roses for last, Hazel knew, so she could judge exactly where to put them for the best effect.

'Lots of people, Hazel. You'd be amazed.'

Hazel *was* amazed. She thought Mr Petrusca had been exaggerating. Surely Mrs Gluck didn't believe there were lots of people like that as well!

'It's true,' said Mrs Gluck.

'Do you know anyone like that?'

'A couple of people.' Mrs Gluck's hands stopped. 'Do you?'

Hazel frowned. 'Who do you know?'

'I wouldn't say, Hazel. If they told me, it's only because they trust me. You see, that's the worst part about it. They're ashamed. They're grown up, and yet they see children reading. It makes them embarrassed. Even though they should ask for help to learn, they don't.'

'And what do you think about people who make fun of people who can't read,' said Hazel, 'or make them feel bad about it?'

'That?' said Mrs Gluck. 'I think that's awful. That's exactly why people don't ask for help, because they're frightened others will make fun of them.' Mrs Gluck put down her flowers and crossed her arms. 'Hazel, that's one of the worst things any person can ever do to another, to stop them asking for help by making them feel embarrassed about needing it. We all need help sometimes—it's *never* something to be ashamed about.' Mrs Gluck shook her head. 'It's a terrible thing to make someone feel like that. It's a sin.'

A sin? Hazel didn't know exactly what a sin was, but she knew it was something very, very bad, much worse than a mistake, or a prank, and maybe even a crime. And yet, that was exactly how she felt about it too.

'And people who do that should be punished, shouldn't they?'

'Well, I don't know about being punished. But they should understand how much pain and suffering they cause. It's a punishment in itself when they realise that.'

'But you shouldn't just forget about it . . . when someone does that.'

'No,' said Mrs Gluck. 'I don't think you should. You should try to make them understand what they've done.'

Hazel nodded. She picked up another marigold. To forget about it—to let the person who had done it get away by pretending it never happened—was the *worst* thing you could do.

13

WHO WAS MR Trimbel's friend, the writer of the code-poem? *He* was the one Hazel had to find.

He lived in the Greville Building. That much Hazel had found out from Mr Petrusca. The Greville Building was five blocks away. It was made out of red and white bricks that had been put together in ridiculous, showy patterns, and it had showy statues of animals all the way around the top, and the people who lived there were showy as well. There had been quite a few fights between children from the Moodey Building and the showy children from the Greville Building over the years. It was always the Greville children's fault, of course, because they were jealous of the Moodeys. It was in the Moodey Building, in a corner apartment on the sixth floor where Mrs Kaspowitz now lived with her son Sergio, that Victor Frogg, the country's greatest prime minister, had been born. The council had even put up a plaque outside Mrs Kaspowitz's door to remind everybody. There were no plaques in the Greville Building—and there was *nothing* the Grevillers could do about that, no matter how showy their building, or how frilly its patterns, or how exquisite and lifelike the statues of the animals around the top. And not only that—the Greville Building was two storeys shorter!

But there must have been hundreds of people living there, almost as many as lived in the Moodey Building, where there were ninety-eight apartments, not counting the basement apartment of Mr Egozian, the caretaker. Just knowing that Mr Trimbel's friend lived in the Greville Building wasn't enough. Hazel needed to know who he was.

Well, there was obviously one person who would know the answer to that particular question! Simple, all she had to do was go to Mr Trimbel and . . .

Go to Mr Trimbel?

This was getting ridiculous. She didn't know where Mr Trimbel lived!

Hazel was sitting in the courtyard of the Moodey Building, where she had gone to think. It was a good, quiet place to think, because hardly anyone ever went there, so no one ever interrupted to ask what you were thinking *about*. Sometimes Mr Egozian came to sweep up. But Mr Egozian never disturbed you. He would sweep quietly, if he saw you were thinking, and go right round you, and come back later to check there was nothing left behind where you had been sitting.

Hazel looked up. On all four sides, rows of windows reached high above her, climbing into the sky. They gazed down at her like dark, unblinking eyes, as if waiting to see what she would do.

Hazel shook her head. It really was ridiculous! She knew Mr Trimbel's name, but she didn't know where he lived. And she knew where his friend lived, but she didn't know his name. Suddenly a strange thought came into her head: it was like a mathematics problem with two unknowns.

Hazel frowned. *A problem with two unknowns?* That was Yak-talk! Half of the Yak's mathematical problems always seemed to be about numbers that he didn't know and which he had to work out. Since he didn't know what they were, he called them 'unknowns'. Solving the problem meant using other information to work out which numbers these unknowns represented. He was *always* talking about them. Sometimes he had two unknowns, and sometimes three, and sometimes four or even more. But you could never work out more than one unknown at a time. You had to work one out after the other, right down to when you only had two, and then— you got a bonus! When you only had two left, you only had to work one of them out, because the last one would follow immediately. That's what the Yak always said, and *logically*, he said, it was always true.

Well, thought Hazel, if I've got two unknowns, I only have to find one. The other one will follow logically. She laughed. If things went on like this, she'd be trying to solve Fermat's Last Theorem next!

How could she solve one of the unknowns? To do that, she needed some other information. Isn't that what the Yak would have said?

To get information, you needed a source. Hazel didn't need the Yak to tell her *that*.

Hazel grinned. A source? She knew the perfect person to talk to. But first, she'd just have to drop in on Mr Volio, to pick up supplies . . .

14

DANIEL, THE BUTCHER'S delivery boy, was sitting on a step at the back of the butcher's shop. His bicycle was leaning against the wall nearby.

Hazel sat down next to him.

Daniel looked at her with a frown. He was a big boy, with curly dark hair and strong arms, and he was already sixteen years old. Mr Lever, the butcher, had promised to take him on as an apprentice in the summer.

'What do you want, little girl?' he asked.

Hazel looked around to see which *little* girl he was talking to.

'Well?'

'Are you having a rest, Daniel?'

'No, I'm riding my bike. Can't you see, Hazel Green?'

'Oh, I thought you might be hungry, so I brought you these. But I suppose, if you're riding your bike, you won't be able to eat them.'

Hazel opened the paper bag she had brought from Mr Volio's bakery. Daniel peered inside.

'Just wait and I'll get off,' said Daniel. He shrugged his shoulders, and moved his arms around, and shook his legs. 'There. I'm off.'

Hazel rolled her eyes.

'Now, what have we got?' said Daniel, looking into the bag again. 'A Chocolate Dipper. Very nice.' He fished it out. 'It's hungry work, Hazel,' said Daniel, 'riding around and delivering packages all day.'

Hazel nodded.

'And Mr Lever makes me carry the carcasses out of the coolroom,' he added proudly. 'He only lets you do that if you're really strong. See.' Daniel leaned forward to show where his white butcher's jacket was stained with the dried blood of the carcasses he had carried over his back. 'Don't be frightened.'

Hazel sighed. It was bad enough having to pretend to wait for him to get off his bike. She wasn't going to pretend to be impressed by a bit of dried blood as well!

Daniel munched his Chocolate Dipper. 'You know what I love about these? The custard,' he said, with his mouth still full. Hazel could see quite a lot of the custard he was talking about.

'So do I,' said Hazel.

'Remember when you stole the secret?' said Daniel, laughing. 'Everyone thought you were the worst sneak they'd ever met.'

'I didn't steal the secret,' said Hazel.

'Didn't you?'

'Don't you ever hear the news?'

'Which news?' said Daniel, finishing the Chocolate

Dipper in one last, enormous mouthful.

'It was Harold.'

'Who's Harold?'

'The apprentice from Mr Volio's bakery.'

Daniel looked at her suspiciously. 'I know you're a very tricky girl, Hazel. Why should I believe you?'

'Do you think Mr Volio would be giving me Chocolate Dippers if I had stolen his secret? Or Cherry Flingers?' she demanded, holding out the bag to Daniel again.

Daniel frowned. 'No. I don't suppose he would. Only don't waste your time trying to trick *me*, Hazel. It won't work.'

Hazel was still holding out the bag. Daniel reached in and took out a Cherry Flinger.

'Do you know Mr Trimbel?' said Hazel, as Daniel bit into the pastry.

'You know what I love about these? The cherries,' he said, showing her a mouthful of them, with a good helping of almond cream as well.

Hazel nodded. 'Do you know Mr Trimbel?' she repeated.

'Mr Trimbel?' said Daniel. 'Let me see. Yes, I know a Mr Trimbel. I took him a delivery yesterday. Or perhaps the day before. Chops. He likes veal chops.'

'Where does he live?'

'I can't tell you where he lives!' Daniel gazed at her with wide eyes. 'What do you think? Do you think I'm just going to tell you something like that?'

'Why not?'

'I can't, that's why not. Mr Lever says we've got a responsibility. Never tell anyone where our customers live, he said to me. The only reason they've told us is so we can make deliveries. If they want someone else to know, they'll tell them themselves.' Daniel paused to see if Hazel understood just how big this responsibility was. 'We're not a public information service. That's another thing Mr Lever says. *Confidentiality*, he calls it. We have to be confident. He told me on the very first day I started doing deliveries, and he repeats it every week, just in case I forget. Never tell where our customers live, how much they pay, or what they buy.'

'Chops,' said Hazel. 'Veal chops. That's what Mr Trimbel buys.'

'How do you know?'

'You told me!'

'*Shhhhhh!*' hissed Daniel, looking around. He whispered: 'I didn't tell you.'

'You did. You just did!'

'*Shhhhh!*'

'Where does he live?'

'I can't tell you. You're so tricky, Hazel Green. I'm not saying anything else to you at all.'

Daniel turned away. He munched more of his Cherry Flinger.

'Look, what harm will it do? You've already told me what he buys, and that's the most *dangerous* information to give away.'

Daniel glanced at her, frowning with uncertainty.

'Of course it is,' said Hazel, 'everyone knows. Compared to that, telling me where he lives doesn't even count.'

Daniel finished his Cherry Flinger. Then he licked the butternut cream off his fingers, which were stained with the dried blood of the carcasses he had carried.

Hazel saw him looking at the bag in her lap. He could eat anything! Didn't Mr Lever let him have lunch? He had already demolished two pastries and still had room for more.

'It's very hungry work . . . all this delivering,' Daniel murmured, glancing hopefully at Hazel.

Hazel handed him the bag. Daniel pulled out a chocolate éclair.

'This is the last one,' he said.

She knew it was the last one. She was the one who'd brought them!

'I suppose you want it?'

Hazel shook her head.

'I suppose we should split it?'

Hazel shook her head again.

'But I'll feel guilty if I eat them all, and you don't get anything.'

No you won't, thought Hazel, not for long.

'All right,' said Daniel, 'if you insist.'

He bit into the éclair. 'You know what I love about these?'

Hazel turned away. She didn't want to see.

'The cream. The cream's always wonderful. Don't you want to try some?'

Hazel could see a bloodstained finger come towards her carrying a big dollop of cream.

'You have it,' she said.

'All right. But you don't know what you're missing.'

It was true. She didn't. Hazel had never tasted a blood-and-cream éclair before.

Daniel licked the cream off his finger and then took another bite of the pastry.

'So you won't be taking anything to Mr Trimbel this evening, then,' she said.

'No,' said Daniel.

'Not going past there?'

'No. Never go past there in the evenings. Not on my route. You can't just go all over the place,' said Daniel, shaking his head. 'You'd never get things done. You have to organise, Hazel. Mr Lever reminds me of that every week as well. I have three routes: morning, afternoon, and evening. In between, when I come back, I carry the carcasses out of the cool room. The evening route's the shortest. I do the part north of Park Street, near the

Burbank and the Fastnet Buildings.'

'Is Mr Trimbel on the afternoon route, then?'

'You won't get it out of me like that. I do the Pollock Building in the *morning*.' Daniel laughed. 'You won't trick me, Hazel Green!'

15

THE POLLOCK BUILDING! That was the first unknown. Now, if the Yak was right, the second unknown, the name of the person who wrote the code-poem, should *logically* follow. All she had to do was go and get it.

Hazel set off for the Pollock Building on Saturday morning. Marcus Bunn saw her as she was leaving, and ran after her.

'I've never been to the Pollock Building,' he said when Hazel told him where she was going, as if that explained why he wanted to come along.

Did Marcus have some kind of list of buildings he needed to visit? 'What about the Syracuse Building?' asked Hazel.

Marcus frowned. 'Where's the Syracuse Building?'

Where's the Syracuse Building? Hazel shook her head, giving Marcus a very curious look.

'I bet you don't know where the Rumble Building is either,' said Hazel, making a name up, just to see what Marcus would do.

'No,' said Marcus.

'If you haven't seen the Rumble Building,' said Hazel, 'I don't know what to say. You *have* to see the Rumble

Building. It durgles there all the time.'

'I see,' said Marcus, nodding his head knowingly. 'Well, I'll certainly try to see it.'

'You should add it to your list,' said Hazel.

Marcus nodded again. Then he stopped. 'What list?'

Hazel didn't reply. If Marcus didn't even know about his own list, there wasn't much point in *her* trying to help him complete it.

They crossed Park Street and headed down Fursten Avenue. Marcus kept talking about the sailing ships that were due in at the port next weekend. They were identical replicas of the sailing ships that were in use two hundred years ago, and they were travelling from port to port all over the world. It was a once-in-a-lifetime chance to see them.

'You could see them in pictures any time,' said Hazel.

'That's not the same, Hazel. These are *real*.'

'Real copies,' said Hazel.

Marcus frowned. 'Well, anyway,' he said eventually, 'we might get to go on them.'

That was better than looking at pictures, Hazel had to admit.

Further down Fursten Avenue they could see a huge barrel suspended high in the air above the pavement. This was the barrel that was attached to the Rum Warehouse, which was an enormous building that had been constructed by merchants to store rum, sugar and cocoa in the days when sailing ships really *were* the only way to cross the seas. But it had long ago ceased to be a merchant's store and now it was an antiques market. Inside, the Rum Warehouse had thick iron columns that rose the height of three storeys and threw beams to one another beneath the roof. This roof was obviously very important because, according to the sign, there were meant to be 200 stalls under it. '200 STALLS UNDER ONE ROOF!' was what the sign said. The sign ran across the front of the building, and above it was the huge barrel, just like one of the wooden rum barrels of old, only thirty times as big. The sign was a big lie. When Hazel had counted the antique stalls in the warehouse, she only got up to 136. Marcus had counted 141, but he admitted that he forgot what number he was up to when he stopped for a donut at the café in the middle of the warehouse. Leon Davis counted 138 and said that Hazel wasn't careful enough. But Abby Simpkin counted 134, and she was the most careful person of all. The most anyone had ever counted was 156, but that was Robert Fischer, who had trouble counting past 20. It was pretty obvious there weren't anywhere *near* 200 stalls, and whenever she passed it Hazel always looked at the sign and thought what a big fat lie it was.

When they reached the Rum Warehouse they went into the entrance under the huge rum barrel. There was plenty of time for them to get to the Pollock Building, and the antique market was always an interesting place to visit. The roof towered high above them. Hazel stopped almost at once in front of a stall with a tall glass cabinet. It contained five shelves crammed full of porcelain brooches with little pictures painted on them. The pictures looked old and faded. A lot of them had red flowers. One had a picture of a small house with a tiny dog sitting in front of it.

Hazel didn't really like brooches like that, not even with tiny dogs on them. Such a tiny dog would have such a tiny bark that it would be of no use at all. It was so ridiculous you just *had* to stop and look at it.

Meanwhile, Marcus had run across and was sitting on a big green sofa at another stall. Marcus loved sitting on the antiques in the Rum Warehouse. He'd try out anything: sofas, armchairs, dining chairs, rocking chairs, benches, stools, ottomans, and even things called chaises, which were half bed and half sofa, with a big curving armrest at one end. He even sat on antique school chairs, although he normally couldn't wait to get away from his own chair at school.

Marcus crossed his arms and beamed smugly at Hazel as she left the brooches stall and crossed the aisle towards him. The light glinted off his glasses. After a minute the stall owner came out and asked him whether he wanted to buy the sofa. From his tone of voice it sounded as if he would be quite surprised if Marcus said yes.

'Oh, don't ask him,' Hazel said seriously to the stall owner. 'He's very irresponsible, and often buys things he doesn't need. He already has four sofas and can't decide which one to sit on first. Come on, Marcus,' she said, 'you don't need another sofa. Let's go and find you a nice dining table.'

Hazel pulled Marcus up. The stall owner crossed his arms and watched them go. Stall owners in the Rum Warehouse were never very welcoming to children. They crossed their arms a lot, and shook their heads a lot, and scowled a lot. That was one of the things that made it so much fun to wander around there. There was one lady who clicked her tongue a lot. She had a tiny stall that sold miniature dolls and antique sewing kits. It was a great mystery to Hazel why anyone would want to buy an antique sewing kit, when you could buy a perfectly good new one, with much nicer cotton, for barely a tenth of the price. Often, as she stood there and wondered, she would hear the lady clicking her tongue behind her.

Once she decided to ask her.

The lady stopped her clicking. She shook her head instead.

'What's your name?' she asked.

'Hazel,' said Hazel.

'Well, Hazel,' said the lady, 'there is nothing on earth more exquisite than an antique doll, especially miniature dolls. And if you have an antique doll, you absolutely must have an antique sewing kit. Does that answer your question?'

Hazel nodded. 'You've taught me a lot.'

The lady smiled. Hazel smiled back. The lady had taught Hazel that she was crazy, because she thought miniature antique dolls were the most exquisite things on earth, that she was illogical, because she said you had to have an antique sewing kit with one, and that she was rude, because she hadn't even given her own name after asking what Hazel was called! This was a lot to find out about someone in the space of three sentences and Hazel couldn't remember ever learning so much as quickly before.

The Rum Warehouse was full of ridiculous things that no one could possibly want to use. That was another thing that made it so much fun. One stall that Hazel knew had a cardboard box full of old rusty bugles. The man who owned the stall said they came from the war. Which war? He picked one up and named a war that Hazel had never even heard of. Abby Simpkin, who knew a lot of history, said this was a war that had happened more than a hundred years before. The next time Hazel went back she asked the man if he would play the bugle.

'These bugles aren't for playing!' he said.

'What are they for, then?' asked Hazel.

'They're antiques,' said the man, as if that were meant to explain it.

As far as Hazel could tell, 'antique' seemed to mean any old thing that people didn't want to use any more. Hazel had some slippers at home that she had grown out of, and supposed that would make them 'antiques' as well. She wondered whether any of the stall keepers would like to sell them.

In the Rum Warehouse, being an 'antique' was an explanation for anything. No matter how silly, old, incomplete or useless an object was, the fact that it was an 'antique' seemed to justify anything.

They walked amongst the stalls. Marcus ran from one sofa to the next, jumping into big plump cushions and letting himself settle comfortably into them. After a while Hazel decided she was going to concentrate on desks. It was often a good idea, she had found from previous visits, to concentrate on one kind of object. That way you could be sure to compare all the different types on display. There were big, flat desks, and desks with slatted roll tops, and desks with little walls of drawers rising up around them. Some were made out of deep, rich coloured woods, and some were made out of lighter, sunnier wood. Some had big squares of blue or green or red leather set into their surfaces, and sometimes there were gold patterns drawn into it. The leather was always cracked, with thousands of tiny crevices running across it like the veins in a leaf. A lot of the desks had ink stains. Eventually Hazel found one with so many ink stains you could barely make out the gold pattern of the leather underneath.

'You'd think they'd clean it up,' said Marcus, who had jumped off the fat ottoman he'd found in the stall next door, and was peering over her shoulder. 'Why would anyone want such a stained old desk?'

'It's an antique,' said Hazel, and they both started laughing.

They were back near the door to the Warehouse. Suddenly Hazel had had enough of antiques for the morning.

'Come on,' she said, 'don't you want to find out why we're going to the Pollock Building?'

16

THE POLLOCK BUILDING wasn't like the Moodey Building at all. It was squat, square and dark. The windows were small. The stone up to the level of the second storey was roughened, which made it seem even stronger and darker.

'It looks like a prison,' whispered Marcus as they stood across the road, gazing at it.

'I think it was a prison once,' said Hazel. 'There are still ghosts in there from the prisoners who died in the dungeons.'

Marcus looked at her in fright. Hazel was glad he was with her. It was always good, she had found in the past, to be with someone who was more frightened than you were. It always made you feel much braver. And if you needed someone like that, you could always depend on Marcus.

They crossed the road.

'I can still turn around and go home, you know,' said Marcus.

'I know.'

'I'm serious. I can, Hazel.'

They were in front of the entrance.

'Well, are you coming in, or not?' demanded Hazel.

Marcus peered through the door, trying to see inside. 'Are we going down to where the dungeons were?'

'That depends whether the person I need to see lives down there,' Hazel said, opening the door.

Cautiously, Marcus followed her in. 'I can still go home,' he whispered.

They were standing in a big lobby. Four leather sofas stood in a square, facing one another. Behind a large wooden counter, a man was watching them. He wore a peaked cap just like an airline pilot, and he wore a smart blue blazer and a blue tie. Altogether, he looked very smart just to be standing behind a counter waiting for people to come through the door.

'Can I help you?' said the man.

Hazel walked up to the counter. 'We're here to see Mr Trimbel,' she said.

'Is he expecting you?'

Hazel frowned. It was very unlikely that Mr Trimbel was expecting her, because she hadn't told anyone she was coming to see him. And yet, sometimes people did discover things that you could never imagine they would have found out. What was the point of asking *her*? Surely the only person who could answer that question was Mr Trimbel himself!

The man behind the desk seemed to be expecting an answer.

'He . . . could be,' she said.

'Could he?' said the man.

'Yes,' said Hazel. It was possible, wasn't it?

'Shall I just check?'

The man picked up a telephone and dialled. Hazel heard someone answer on the other end.

'Hello, Mr Trimbel? There's a girl and boy here to see you. They say you're expecting them.'

You say he's expecting us, thought Hazel. I only said he could be.

The man turned back to Hazel. 'Mr Trimbel doesn't think he's expecting you.'

'He might have forgotten,' said Hazel.

'You might have forgotten, Mr Trimbel.' The man listened. 'He doesn't think he's forgotten,' he said to Hazel. 'Are you sure it's today?'

'Of course it's today,' said Hazel. That was a very strange question. When was it ever *not* today? A man who asked questions like that could easily forget when he had been expecting someone. 'He'll probably remember when he sees us,' said Hazel.

'You'll probably remember when you see them,' said the man into the telephone. He listened. He nodded. Then he hung up. 'Mr Trimbel says he'd better see you,' he said. 'His apartment is 404.'

'That isn't downstairs . . . in the dungeons, is it?' whispered Marcus.

Hazel grinned. 'Don't worry about him,' she said to the man. 'He thinks this used to be a prison.'

The man laughed. He took off his hat. 'You shouldn't believe everything people say, kid,' he said.

'Exactly,' said Hazel. 'That's what I keep telling him. If I wasn't there to stop him, he could easily have bought a sofa this morning, you know. Maybe even two.' Hazel leaned forward and lowered her voice, as if it were a secret between herself and the man in the blazer. 'He doesn't need any more sofas. But he likes to sit on them.'

'Really? Do you like to sit on sofas, kid?'

'Yes,' said Marcus, 'especially the ones with really thick cushions.'

'You see,' whispered Hazel.

The man nodded.

'Apartment 404?' said Hazel.

'What? Oh, yes. The elevator's over there.'

'Thank you,' said Hazel. 'We won't be long.'

'Take your time!' said the man, grinning, and he put his hat back on his head.

'Hazel,' said Marcus, when they were in the elevator, '*you* told me this used to be a prison.'

'I know.'

'But it wasn't, was it?'

Hazel shrugged. 'That man doesn't think so, but he says you can't believe everything people tell you. So I don't see why you should believe *him*.'

'Yes,' said Marcus, nodding his head thoughtfully, 'I suppose that's true. I wonder who you can believe?'

The elevator stopped at the fourth floor. They got out.

'Hazel,' said Marcus.

'Yes?'

'This Mr Trimbel . . . he *isn't* expecting us, is he?'

'I don't see how he could be,' said Hazel. 'But he seems to think he may have forgotten.'

Mr Trimbel peered at Hazel and Marcus. He had thick glasses that made his eyes look bigger than they were.

'Mr Trimbel?' said Hazel.

'Yes,' said Mr Trimbel cautiously.

'We're the girl and boy from downstairs, the ones you were talking about on the phone just before.'

'Yes,' said Mr Trimbel.

'Can we come in, please?'

Mr Trimbel hesitated. He was wearing a soft plum-coloured jacket, with a green velvet waistcoat underneath. He looked up and down the corridor, as if to see whether anyone else were watching.

'All right,' he said.

Mr Trimbel closed the door behind them. For a moment, he looked as if he didn't know what to do with them. He peered at them again with his magnified eyes.

'I don't think I was expecting you,' he said. 'I rarely forget when I'm expecting someone.'

'That's all right,' said Hazel. 'We don't mind not being expected. Do we, Marcus?'

Marcus shook his head. He was gazing at Mr Trimbel's big eyes. Mr Trimbel glanced at him and gave a little jump of surprise when he noticed Marcus watching him so closely.

'Well, I suppose you'd better . . . come this way.'

Mr Trimbel led them into a small room with a dining table and six chairs. The chairs had high, straight backs. The wallpaper was dark red with a pattern of little leaf-like spikes. There was nothing else in the room, just the table and chairs, and one picture on the wall showing cows grazing under a dark, cloudy sky. Mr Trimbel's whole apartment was very neat, with hardly a thing out of place, and not many things to get out of place anyway!

They sat down on the straight, stiff chairs. Mr Trimbel glanced at Marcus again. Marcus pursed his lips and sucked in his cheeks, and put a very thoughtful look on his face, as if he were thinking about the very important reason they had come unexpectedly to visit Mr Trimbel. He had no idea what it was, of course, because Hazel hadn't told him.

'Mr Trimbel,' said Hazel suddenly, 'I understand you like lobsters.'

Mr Trimbel thought about that. 'It depends what you mean by "like",' he said eventually. 'For instance, would I like to go to the theatre with one? No. Or would I like to introduce one to my friends? No. On the other hand—'

Mr Trimbel stopped. Marcus was laughing. He frowned.

'Is something funny, young man?'

Marcus stared in confusion. 'I thought . . . you were . . . wasn't it a joke?'

'What?'

'The bit about going to a theatre with a lobster.'

Mr Trimbel thought about it. 'No, I said I *wouldn't* go to the theatre with a lobster. The joke would be if I said I would. That would be quite funny.'

'Don't worry about him,' said Hazel. 'What I mean is: you like to eat them, don't you?'

'It's true,' replied Mr Trimbel. 'I do like to eat lobster. A fine lobster, with a fine white wine, children, is the finest dish imaginable. At least, that's my opinion.' Mr Trimbel frowned. 'I don't suppose I should talk about wine, should I? You're too young to drink wine, I think.' He peered at them again, as if he wasn't sure how old they were, or when a child could start to drink wine, or anything at all about children, if it came to that.

'Don't worry, you can talk about it, Mr Trimbel,' said Hazel. 'People talk about all kinds of things. My aunt's always talking about the way Uncle Archie crashed their car, and no one's meant to crash a car, no matter how old they are.'

128

'I never drive,' said Mr Trimbel.

'But you drink wine?'

'Yes . . .' Mr Trimbel said cautiously.

'With lobster?'

'Oh, yes. Only the finest wine will do!'

'Well, that's why we're here,' said Hazel. 'It's about lobsters.'

'Is it?' whispered Marcus, 'not those lobsters Mr Pet—'

Hazel gave Marcus a quick elbow in the ribs. Mr Trimbel raised his eyebrows.

'You were going to get a pair of lobsters from Mr Petrusca a while ago.'

'Yes,' said Mr Trimbel. 'I always used to get my lobsters from Mr Petrusca, until, well . . . he *disappointed* me recently.'

'I know,' said Hazel.

'Do you? I was supposed to get two extremely excellent lobsters from him, and yet, when I went to collect them, they gave me two quite . . . ordinary lobsters. *Quite* ordinary!'

'The others were stolen,' said Hazel.

'Yes, I heard that, but I find it hard to believe.'

'You don't think Mr Petrusca would lie!'

'I didn't say he lied,' said Mr Trimbel quickly. 'I'm very particular about things like that. I would *never* accuse anybody if I didn't have solid proof.' He glanced at Marcus. 'Did I say he lied, young man?'

Marcus frowned, thinking. 'No, I don't think he did, Hazel.'

'Exactly. I simply said it was hard to believe. The truth is often hard to believe, much harder, in many cases, than fiction.'

'Mr Trimbel, I saw those lobsters. They were the biggest lobsters you can imagine.' Hazel stretched out her arms as far as they would go. 'They were *this* big.'

'Then they must have been alligators, not lobsters,' said Mr Trimbel, peering at the gap between Hazel's hands.

'Well, they may not have been *that* big. But that's how they looked, Mr Trimbel, because there never was a bigger lobster ever. Kings of lobsters, they were. And do you know what Mr Petrusca fed them?'

'No,' said Mr Trimbel, leaning forward to find out.

'Sea urchin and Barbary squid!'

'Barbary squid . . .' murmured Mr Trimbel dreamily.

'And sea urchin!'

'Oh, what happened to them?' cried Mr Trimbel in anguish, as if he had just left behind a dream to find himself in a nightmare. 'Where did they go? Who took them?'

'Well, that's just it, Mr Trimbel,' said Hazel. 'That's why we've come. We need your help to find the thief.'

'Of course, of course. My help.' He glanced at Marcus. 'That's what you need, isn't it?'

Marcus shrugged.

'What can I do?' demanded Mr Trimbel.

'We need a name,' said Hazel.

Suddenly Mr Trimbel was quiet. He sat up straight again, as straight as he could sit in his straight-backed seat. He gazed at Hazel through his thick glasses.

'Do you know who took them?' he asked.

'I just need a name.'

'Whose name?'

'Your friend's name. The one you were supposed to have the lobsters with.'

Mr Trimbel gasped. 'What are you saying? Are you saying my friend took them?'

Hazel didn't answer straight away. Mr Trimbel didn't look happy. But was he angry at his friend, for having stolen the lobsters—or at Hazel, for having accused him?

He was glaring at her, and because of the magnifying lenses in his glasses, this gave him twice as much glare as Hazel had ever seen before.

'Maybe we should go, Hazel,' whispered Marcus.

'What are you saying?' demanded Mr Trimbel again. 'Are you accusing my friend?'

This time Hazel wasn't in any doubt. Marcus was shifting to the very edge of his seat, getting ready to run.

'I'm not accusing him,' said Hazel. 'I just want his name so he can help us as well.'

'Where's the proof? Well, where is it?'

It was right there in Hazel's pocket, the code-poem

that Mr Trimbel's friend had written. But she couldn't show it to Mr Trimbel, because then he would ask why Mr Petrusca hadn't given it to him in the first place . . . and there would be no way to answer *that* question without telling the whole world Mr Petrusca's secret.

'Well? You're lying, aren't you? Lying!'

By now Marcus was on his feet. Hazel got up as well.

'Go on. Go on, out you go! I never want to see you again.'

'I'm not lying!' cried Hazel in reply.

'I *wasn't* expecting you, was I? Go on, out you go!' said Mr Trimbel.

Marcus was already out in the hallway and racing for the door. Hazel ran after him.

'I'm not lying,' she cried one last time, stopping at the door. 'You'll see I'm not.'

'Out! Out with you!' cried Trimbel, coming out of the dining room and waving his arms.

Marcus was already at the elevator, jabbing and re-jabbing the button. They waited breathlessly for the doors to open. Mr Trimbel stood and glared at them from his apartment door until the elevator arrived.

When they came out into the lobby, the man behind the counter was on the phone. He dropped it and started to shout as soon as he saw them. They ran straight out and kept on running.

They didn't stop until they reached the Rum

Warehouse. Only then did they dare to look back to see if the man in the peaked cap had followed them.

They leaned against a wall, catching their breath. Marcus took his glasses off and his rosy cheeks were rosier than ever.

'That wasn't very much fun,' he said eventually.

'I'm sorry,' said Hazel, 'but I didn't say it was going to be fun.'

'No, that's true, you didn't,' said Marcus, who always tried to be fair. 'I should have asked you before.'

'That's right,' said Hazel.

'Why do you care so much about these lobsters?'

'I don't care about the *lobsters*,' said Hazel. Marcus was beginning to sound just like Leon Davis!

'Really? It sounded like you did.'

Two men were bringing a piano out of a big van. Hazel and Marcus watched as the men rolled it down some planks on a flat trolley with tiny little wheels and pushed it into the Rum Warehouse.

Suddenly Marcus laughed. 'He was very angry, that Mr Trimbel, when you started lying about his friend!'

'I wasn't lying! Anyway, you didn't think it was so funny at the time, Marcus Bunn.'

'Well, it wasn't as funny at the time as it is now.'

True, thought Hazel, things are often funnier after they've happened.

'Mr Trimbel didn't tell you what you wanted to find out, did he?' said Marcus.

Yes, it was very clever of Marcus to have noticed.

'So what are you going to do now?'

Hazel didn't reply. That was the best question Marcus had asked all day!

'Maybe you'll never find out,' said Marcus, and he started walking home.

17

IT WOULD HAVE been easy to give up. After all, no one else even knew that Hazel was looking for the person who had stolen Mr Petrusca's lobsters. It would have been easy, very easy, to give up, and perhaps a lot of other people would have done just that. But not Hazel Green.

Hazel walked past the fish shop. It was busy. There was Mr Petrusca, behind the counter, filleting a fish. His head was lowered as he worked. Hazel stopped and watched through the window. Now he was wrapping the fish in paper. He reached forward and handed it to his customer. Then he turned to someone else, who pointed at the counter, and a moment later he was pulling another fish off a tray, holding it out on the palm of his hand while the customer decided whether she wanted it.

There he was, *pretending*. Meanwhile, whoever had stolen the lobsters, whoever had written that note, was still out there. He was getting away scot-free.

Logically, thought Hazel, her plan should have worked. When you had two unknowns, and you found one, the second was meant to follow immediately. Well, the second *hadn't* followed immediately—and the Yak had better be able to explain why!

*

The Yak's mother opened the door. She was wearing a silk gown the colour of freshly mown grass, and her fingernails were painted green as well. Her shoes were a dark blue, like a very deep lake. In one hand she was holding a necklace of lacquer, as if she had just been about to put it on when Hazel knocked. The colour of her hair was as light as fine sand.

'Are you looking for Yakov?'

'Yes,' said Hazel.

The Yak's mother held up the necklace. She glanced at Hazel, her eyebrows arched in a question. Hazel peered at the necklace, studying it carefully. Each piece was intricately carved into the shape of a beautiful flower. But perhaps that was just a little *too* intricate, almost as if the craftsman had been showing off.

Hazel wasn't sure. She looked back at the Yak's mother and shrugged.

'Yes,' said the Yak's mother, sighing. 'That's just what I was thinking.'

The Yak came into the front room. This time Hazel had selected a sofa with a pattern of orange and cream. Sometimes Hazel thought she should bring Marcus Bunn along with her just once so he could test out all the sofas and armchairs that stood around her. But he was so jealous, she didn't know what he might do. He might go bouncing around in his shoes until he had broken all the springs.

'Hello,' said the Yak.

'Hello.'

'I saw you from my window the other day,' said the Yak.

'Did you? What was I doing?'

'You were in the courtyard. You looked like you were thinking.' The Yak grinned.

'I *was* thinking,' said Hazel, 'about a problem.'

'Don't tell me! I bet Mrs Nimsky's cousin decided he didn't want the farm after all, even though he said he'd buy it.'

Hazel shook her head.

'Then he's lost the money, hasn't he? He's gambled it away!'

'It's got nothing to do with the Nimskies. I was thinking about something that's just like a mathematical problem.'

The Yak looked at her disbelievingly. 'What kind of mathematical problem?'

'A mathematical problem with two unknowns.'

The Yak gazed at Hazel suspiciously. It *sounded* like a mathematical problem.

'It's got two unknowns. Only with this problem, when you work out one unknown, the second doesn't follow. Even though a certain person is always telling me that logically the last unknown *has* to follow.'

The Yak frowned. 'Are you sure it doesn't?'

'Very sure.' Hazel gazed hard at the Yak. 'Very, *very* sure.'

The Yak shifted uncomfortably in his seat. 'You'd better tell me about it.'

Hazel nodded. 'There's a person called Mr Trimbel, and he has a friend—'

'Hazel, I thought this was a mathematical problem with two unknowns.'

'It is,' Hazel said sternly, 'just listen. There's a person called Mr Trimbel and he has a friend, but I don't know what he's called. That's the first unknown.'

'I see,' said the Yak, 'let's call him X.'

'It's very unlikely that would be his name, Yakov. I've never heard of anyone called X.'

'No, you always call the first unknown X.'

'All right,' said Hazel. She hardly ever did anything because people *always* did it, but when it came to mathematics, the Yak was the expert! 'So there's this person called X, who's Mr Trimbel's friend. Now, I know where X lives, the Greville Building. But I didn't know where Mr Trimbel lives, so that was the second unknown.'

'Y,' said the Yak.

'Well, because I didn't know it.'

'No, Y. You call the second unknown Y.'

Hazel sighed. This was getting quite confusing—and they hadn't even started trying to solve the problem! 'All right,' she said, 'you can call it whatever you like. The point is I didn't know where Mr Trimbel lived and that was the second unknown.'

'Yes,' said the Yak. 'It is quite mathematical. Now, what you have to do is to work out Y. After that—'

'I know that,' said Hazel. Who did the Yak think he was talking to? 'That's what I was working out when you saw me sitting in the courtyard. And I *have* found Y.'

'And? What is it?'

'The Pollock Building. That's where Mr Trimbel lives.'

'Then you've solved the problem! The last unknown will follow logically.'

'Not in this case. This particular unknown didn't *want* to tell me what the last unknown was.'

The Yak frowned. 'I've never heard of unknowns doing that before,' he murmured. 'I don't *think* they're meant to have a choice.'

'This one did. You see, although Mr Trimbel knows who X is, he won't say.'

'How do you know?'

'I asked him!'

'This is very irregular,' said the Yak. 'I've never found a problem you can't solve when you've just got one unknown left.'

Hazel shrugged. The Yak sat back in his chair and thought. He gazed at the table for a long time, and bunched up his nose in concentration, as if he had a pea stuck inside. Finally he looked back at Hazel. 'All I can tell you is that when you try one approach to solve a problem, and it doesn't work, the best way is to try another. That's a good principle and I think you should use it.'

'How?'

'Well, Mr Trimbel isn't a very helpful unknown, is he?'

'No. He's the most unhelpful unknown I've ever met!'

'Exactly. So let's forget him. That leaves us with X, whose name we still don't know, and where X lives, which we *do* know.'

'Correct,' said Hazel, wondering what was going on inside the Yak's brain.

'So we've got one known, and one unknown. That's not enough. You've always got to have more knowns than unknowns. If we had *two* knowns, then we might be able to solve it.' The Yak peered at Hazel. 'Is there anything else you know about X? Think hard. Take your time. *Anything?*'

But Hazel didn't need to take any time at all. 'Yes,' she said immediately. 'He wrote the code you deciphered.'

18

'HAZEL,' SAID THE Yak, 'what is this all about?'

'I can't say,' said Hazel.

'That was a very strange poem. It was about lobster dinners, wasn't it? Why do you want to meet the person who wrote it?'

'I won't be meeting anyone unless I can work out his name. Come on, Yakov, how can we do it?'

The Yak glanced at her, as if wondering whether he should help. Then he shook his head, and gave a sigh.

'All right.'

'Good! Come on, what should we do?'

'Shhhh. Just let me think.'

And that was what the Yak did, gazing vacantly at the table, sometimes frowning, sometimes smiling, then suddenly shaking his head, and screwing up his nose, and frowning again. After a while Hazel began to wonder *what* he was thinking about. You had to be very careful with the Yak. He could hardly go for five minutes without starting to think about one of his mathematical problems, even when he was meant to be concentrating on something else. It was like a sickness. And now that Hazel knew he sometimes played the violin in his head, there was something else she had to watch out for.

'I've got it!'

Hazel looked up with a start.

'This is what you have to do. X wrote the poem, correct?'

Hazel nodded.

'Now, it wasn't a particularly hard code, just a rule of threes, but not many people would be able to crack it. On average, I'd say, if you took a hundred people on the street, the only one who'd be able to make any sense of it would be the one who wrote it.'

'Only if he was on the street at the time,' said Hazel, grinning, thinking it was a joke.

But it wasn't a joke.

'Exactly,' said the Yak. 'If you stood on the street with something written in that code, and someone could actually read it, you could be sure it was him. Well, pretty sure. In fact, I'd say the probability would be . . .' the Yak paused for a moment, calculating in his head, '. . . 99.76%.'

'But what are the chances of that person just happening to walk past you on the street?' demanded Hazel.

'Quite high—if you're standing outside the building where he lives.'

'Outside the Greville Building?' said Hazel.

'Precisely,' said the Yak.

He smiled smugly, as smugly, thought Hazel, as a mathematical cat who'd just lapped up a bowl of milk.

But there was something Hazel didn't particularly like about the Yak's plan. It meant standing outside the Greville Building while people walked in and out. And not only that, it meant standing there carrying something . . . some kind of . . . what? What would she have to carry?

'A sign,' said the Yak. 'Or a placard. Written in the code.'

'A placard?' said Hazel. 'People will laugh.' She thought about all the showy Grevillers who were always fighting with the Moodey children. They'd laugh more than anyone!

'Why will they laugh?'

'Because I'll be standing there with a placard with a whole lot of rubbish written on it.'

'It won't be rubbish,' said the Yak stiffly. 'It will be a perfectly sensible message in code.'

'In a perfectly ridiculous code.'

'It's quite a clever code. I bet lots of people will stand around trying to decipher it.'

'I don't think so, Yakov,' said Hazel.

'I would, if I saw something like that on the street.'

That was why Hazel didn't think so.

'There must be another way,' she said.

The Yak shrugged. 'That's the only one I can think of. Unless you have another idea . . .'

Hazel didn't have another idea. She leaned back in her

armchair and put her hands behind her head. She looked up at the ceiling. There was a lovely chandelier hanging there. She wished someone would turn it on so she could see the light glint and sparkle.

'So what do we write?' she asked.

'First of all, it has to be in the code. It doesn't matter so much what it says, because only the person who wrote the code will understand it. Whoever can read it—*whatever* it says—is the person you want.'

'But it should say something sensible. It shouldn't just say "Fresh Goldfish for Fifteen Cents".'

The Yak frowned. 'Goldfish cost more than that, don't they?'

It had to say something to make Mr Trimbel's friend feel guilty, thought Hazel. 'It should say something like: *You're a nasty man with horrible ideas.*'

'What about: *You're a nasty man with a horrible plan?*'

'Yes,' cried Hazel. 'A rhyme. Just like *he* wrote!'

The Yak nodded. He ran out to get some paper.

'Listen, listen!' said Hazel as soon as he got back. *'You're a nasty man with a horrible plan, and you should join your lobsters in the frying pan.'*

'No, Hazel,' said the Yak. 'First we have to plan what we're going to say. How many verses do we want? How many lines should each verse have? Do we want to rhyme every line in each verse, or every second line? Do we use the present tense or the past? Do we speak in the first person or the third? Do we speak in the singular or the plural? Do we . . . What? What is it?'

Hazel was staring at the Yak. *What was he doing?* Suddenly, everything had become complicated. This was worse than doing composition for school! The Yak's problem, thought Hazel, as she had often thought before, was that he liked order. But writing poems was *chaos*.

'What is it?' said the Yak again.

'Yakov, write this: *You're . . . a . . . nasty . . .*'

The Yak hadn't started.

'Write, Yakov Plonsk!' said Hazel, and she fixed him with one of her fearful glances. In fact, the glance coming out of her eyes was so strong, and so powerful, that she could almost feel her eyeballs being pushed backwards in her head.

The Yak began to write.

'*You're . . . a . . . nasty . . .*'

'I've done that.'

'*. . . man . . . with a horrible plan . . . and you should join your . . . lobsters . . . in the frying pan.*' Then Hazel paused, thinking about the next line. '*The thing you did was thoroughly naughty, and you've left Mr Petrusca . . . Mr Petrusca . . . wondering why.*'

'No,' said the Yak, 'that doesn't work.'

'Of course it works. "Naughty"—"Why". They both end in Y.'

'They don't rhyme, Hazel.'

'Well, they should.'

'There once was a girl who said "They should", but her rhymes hardly ever sounded good.'

'Very funny,' said Hazel. *'The thing you did was thoroughly awful . . . thoroughly mean . . . The thing you did was thoroughly mean, and Mr Petrusca feels like a bean.'*

'And what does a bean feel like?'

'Unhappy,' said Hazel. 'Obviously.'

The Yak was gazing at her with his eyebrows raised. He didn't look completely convinced.

'Some beans,' Hazel explained. 'Not all of them. One or two might be happy. But most of them are sad.'

'Well, how about: *The thing you did was thoroughly bad, and you've left Mr Petrusca feeling sad?'*

'Yes,' said Hazel. 'As sad as a bean. Isn't that what I said?'

The Yak was writing. When he finished he held up the piece of paper and solemnly cleared his throat.

> *'You're a nasty man with a horrible plan,*
> *And you should join your lobsters in the frying pan.*
> *The thing you did was thoroughly bad,*
> *And you've left Mr Petrusca feeling sad.'*

'Perfect!' said Hazel. 'Can you put that into the code?'
The Yak nodded.

'And then I'll make a placard. And after that, we just have to go to the Greville Building and stand outside.'

The Yak stared at her. 'We? *We* have to go to the Greville Building?'

'Hazel Green!' exclaimed the Yak. 'I've done what you asked. You had a mathematical problem and I've helped you solve it.'

'Incorrect,' said Hazel, trying to sound as mathematical as possible. 'You've helped me *think* of a way to solve it. But you haven't *actually* solved it yet. It will only be solved when we know who X is. What kind of a mathematician gives up on a problem halfway through?'

'I'm not giving up—'

'Not a very respectable one, that's what I would say.'

The Yak gazed suspiciously at Hazel.

'Besides,' said Hazel, 'what happens if Mr X starts talking in code? I wouldn't know what he was saying. Only you would.'

'Hazel, that's ridiculous. No one *talks* in code. Code is only something you write.'

'Drrribell!'

'What?'

'That's code. Sometimes I talk in it. It means "rubbish"!'

The Yak folded his arms in despair.

'Don't you remember the time you helped me catch the apprentices, Yakov? You loved that.'

'I didn't *love* it . . . Anyway, that was real detective work. That was like being a spy. You almost had to be invisible.'

That's right, thought Hazel, which is why the Yak had turned up in broad daylight dressed completely in black, with a black balaclava, which made him the most visible 'invisible' spy who ever lived.

'This is detective work as well,' she said. 'Only you don't need to be invisible,' Hazel added quickly, in case he was thinking of getting out his balaclava again.

'Well, if I did agree to go,' said the Yak after a moment, 'you'd have to tell me everything about it, exactly why you need to find Mr X.'

'I can't.'

The Yak shrugged.

'It's a secret.'

'I can keep a secret. All mathematicians—'

'Yes, I know, all mathematicians can keep secrets.'

Mathematicians could do anything, if you listened to the Yak. Hazel paused to think. It was a big secret, perhaps the most important one Hazel had ever been told, but the Yak *would* keep it. She was sure of it. And it *would* be good to have someone with her when she unmasked Mr X. You never knew what might happen. He might try to make a run for it, or barricade himself in his apartment and not come out until they broke his door down!

'All right, Yakov,' said Hazel eventually. 'But you have to swear.'

'No, Hazel, I hate—'

'Swear on your nose! Swear you'll never tell anyone what you're about to hear.'

'It's ridiculous!' cried the Yak. 'It's just so ridiculous.'

It was ridiculous, that was the whole point. To swear on your nose, for the Moodey children, was the biggest test, the most solemn oath, and no one would *dare* to misuse it.

'I'm serious, Yakov. This is a big secret. I wouldn't tell it to anybody else, even if they did swear. It's only because I trust you so much.'

The Yak frowned. She always wanted him to swear on his nose, and he always felt foolish when he did it. It was the most illogical, irrational, *unmathematical* thing he ever had to do. Deep down, he always wondered whether she were making fun of him.

But Hazel wasn't making fun of him. She was absolutely serious.

The Yak put his finger to his nose. 'I swear never to tell anyone what I'm about to hear.' He whipped his finger away as quickly as he could. 'Well?'

'It's about Mr Petrusca,' said Hazel, and she leaned forward and whispered the whole story, about the lobsters, and the note, and everything that had happened, and everything Mr Petrusca had told her about himself.

And she told how she had vowed to find the person who was responsible, and make him realise what he had done!

The Yak listened in silence. When Hazel finished he thought about what she had told him.

'All right,' he said eventually, 'I'll come with you. On Saturday.'

'Good. We'll go at ten—' Suddenly Hazel stopped. 'Oh, I've forgotten. I can't go on Saturday, Yakov.'

'Why not?'

'I can't.'

The Yak stared at her.

'I really can't. I've got to go with . . . I mean I've got to go and see . . . there are some ships . . .' Hazel's voice trailed off.

'Ships?' said the Yak.

'Sailing ships,' whispered Hazel.

'And you're telling me that's more important than finding Mr X? After you come to me and ask to help solve the problem? After you accuse *me* of giving up halfway through? After you *vowed* to solve it?'

It did sound ridiculous, when you put it like that. And it would sound even more ridiculous if she explained that the reason she had to go was to mill around with all the Moodey children against people from other buildings. It *wasn't* ridiculous—but the Yak, who was the sort of person who walked to and from school all by himself, wouldn't understand. And the more she tried to explain it to him, she knew, the less he would be willing to accept it.

'Saturday,' said the Yak. 'I'll translate the message into the code. You make the placard.'

Hazel nodded. She winced. She could just imagine what everyone would say about her when she didn't turn up on Saturday . . . Leon Davis loudest of all!

Well, at least the Greville children would be away seeing the ships. That was one advantage. They wouldn't be there to laugh at her while she was carrying the *Drrribell* placard in front of their building.

19

ON SATURDAY MORNING Hazel waited inside. With luck, everyone would go off to the ships before they even realised she was missing. Of course, she didn't really believe that would happen. Things were never that easy. When the doorbell rang, she knew exactly who it would be.

'Marcus!'

'What are you doing, Hazel? Everyone's ready to go. We're all waiting downstairs.'

Cobbler was with him, and Mandy Furstow as well. They both nodded.

'I'm not going,' said Hazel.

Marcus stared at her in amazement.

'I don't think the ships are there,' she said.

'Of course they're there!'

'No, I think there was a storm. They've been delayed.'

Marcus, Cobbler and Mandy all looked at each other.

'I haven't heard about a storm,' said Mandy.

'Well, I'm not completely sure,' said Hazel. Storms *did* happen, and ships *were* delayed, and it always took a while to find out. So it *was* possible.

'Leon Davis is down there,' said Marcus. 'And everyone else. We're all ready.'

Hazel nodded. There was nothing she could do. She couldn't go, and she couldn't tell them the reason.

Marcus was still staring at her. Cobbler and Mandy were already going back to the elevator. Cobbler was shaking his head, and Mandy threw a disappointed glance over her shoulder at Hazel.

'What are you going to do instead?' asked Marcus suspiciously.

'Nothing,' said Hazel.

'Maybe I'll stay and do nothing as well.'

'No, Marcus, you need to go.'

'Why?'

'Well, we need all the Moodey people we can get.'

'But I thought you said the ships weren't there.'

'But what if the Grevillers are there?'

'Then we need you as well!'

'Look, Marcus, just go! I can't come. That's all there is to it!'

'You *can't* come?' whispered Marcus.

The elevator had arrived. Cobbler and Mandy were waiting for him.

'Just go, Marcus, please,' Hazel whispered. 'I'll explain another time.'

'When?'

'I don't know.' Hazel started pushing him. 'Please, Marcus, please.'

'All right,' said Marcus. 'But don't think you're fooling

me. When Leon Davis starts calling you names, don't expect me to stand up for you. And if he decides to tell everyone you preferred to visit the Yak, well . . . well . . .' spluttered Marcus, his face growing redder, his eyes flashing brighter, '. . . don't expect *me* to defend you!'

The Yak had never seen the Greville Building before. Hazel warned him that it was very showy and so he shouldn't expect to like it. But the Yak thought it was very interesting, and he stood gazing up at the animals on the top for a long time, saying how wonderful he thought they looked. According to the Yak, the proportions were almost perfect. Eventually Hazel found herself gazing at them as well. They *were* quite wonderful, she found herself thinking, before she remembered they were on top of the Greville Building, and therefore couldn't be *that* wonderful.

'Come on,' she said, 'we're not here for sightseeing. We've got work to do.'

Hazel was carrying a stick, to which she had attached the placard with the Yak's code translation of their poem. The Yak had dressed especially in a grey, speckled jacket and an orange tie.

'You look ridiculous,' Hazel had said when she saw him.

'I do not look ridiculous. I'm dressed as a detective. This is a houndstooth jacket, exactly like detectives wear.'

'Houndstooth? You mean, like the fangs on an

Alsatian?' said Hazel, and she threw out her hand towards the Yak's throat.

The Yak jumped away.

'And what's the tie for?' said Hazel.

'There'll be code-breakers there today, Hazel. I have to look respectable. I'm a mathematician!'

Hazel sighed. There was always something new to learn about mathematicians from the Yak, and their funny ideas about clothes was only the latest discovery. She just hoped he didn't have a houndstooth balaclava stuffed in his pocket!

'Well,' said Hazel, drawing a deep breath. 'I suppose we should get started.'

The Yak nodded. Hazel glanced around. She still felt silly at the idea of holding up a placard with such nonsense on it, even if the nonsense concealed a very clever, very *chaotic* poem underneath.

She took one last look around, then raised the placard in the air.

The placard was a powerful object. It exerted a strange effect on people. For a start, it made them stop. Then it made them frown. Then it made them shake their heads. Then it made them smile. All around Hazel, people stopped, frowned, shook their heads, and smiled. Some of them even started chuckling. And all of this because of something they couldn't even understand!

Another power of the placard was to drive people away. People walked in a *big* circle around Hazel, as if afraid to get too close. Even when they stopped to frown at it, they didn't approach her, but stared from a distance, before they walked off, shaking their heads and chuckling. You might easily have imagined they thought the placard—and the girl who was holding it—was not only slightly mad, but dangerous!

All of this was so unusual that after a few moments Hazel decided to test it. She put the sign down to see what would happen. People began to walk around her as normal. She put it up. *Bang!* Big empty circle around her, people stopping and then rushing away.

The placard was the most powerful thing she had ever held in her hands, and it was only a piece of cardboard!

'This is amazing,' she whispered to the Yak.

The Yak didn't reply. He was gazing at the animals on top of the building again.

'Yakov,' she whispered.

'Do you realise?' said the Yak. 'If you put the weight of two of those animals on one end of a beam fifteen metres long, and placed the other end—'

'Yakov! You're meant to be watching for someone who's breaking the code. I don't think any of those animals—'

Hazel froze. Someone had just touched her shoulder.

'Let me see that!' said a voice.

It must be Mr X!

Hazel turned around.

If it was Mr X, he had even stranger ideas about clothes than the Yak. He was wearing a white suit and a hat that looked like a hamburger, with a big plastic pickle stuck on the top. He had a sandwich board over his shoulders and it had a sign which said 'EAT AT BENNY'S! HAMBURGERS $2.50. SHAKES 99c. EAT AT BENNY'S!'

'Where's Benny's?' said the Yak.

The man growled. 'That's my patch over there,' he said to Hazel, pointing down the street. 'You come down there, and you're in trouble! Let's see what your sign says, anyway.'

He peered at Hazel's placard.

'You really should put Benny's address on your board,' said the Yak. 'I wouldn't know where to go even if I *did* want to eat at Benny's.'

'Hah! You'll never sell any of that around here,' said the man, throwing a hand up dismissively. Then he turned around and stomped away, shrugging his shoulders to adjust his sandwich board, which had slipped down on one side.

'Sell any of what?' asked Hazel, and both she and the Yak looked at the placard, to work out what the man had been talking about.

Hazel raised the placard again. People came and went around her. She scanned their faces as they approached, looking to see if they understood the sign. Could this man in the grey suit be Mr X, for instance . . . or this old gentleman shuffling along in a brown cardigan and baggy trousers? He looked like just the kind of man to write codes—but he didn't look like the kind of man to go on a daring raid to steal a pair of lobsters. He stopped, frowned, smiled a little, shook his head and shuffled on. No, thought Hazel, and she looked around to see who else was coming towards her.

Still Mr X didn't appear. Down the street, the man with the sandwich board walked up and down, and Hazel could see him glancing at her with a scowling look on his face. The time passed slowly. Now and again Hazel thought she recognised someone who had already stopped to look at the placard earlier, but there were so many people that it was hard to be sure. Besides, once she had been there for a while she was bound to start seeing people coming *and* going.

Hazel began to wonder whether the plan was going to work. How long was she going to stand there? After all, there was no guarantee that Mr X would see her. There might even be a back entrance to the Greville Building. Since he was the kind of person who crept around stealing lobsters, that was probably the type of entrance he'd *prefer* to use.

In the meantime, the Yak had moved away. He wandered amongst the people, peering around their shoulders. 'I'm on surveillance,' he whispered confidentially, when he came back to Hazel for a moment, 'I'm looking to see if any of them are writing it down and deciphering it,' and off he went again, raising his shoulders and burying his chin deep in the lapels of his houndstooth jacket.

He was off on one of his surveillances when Michael Drummond turned the corner.

Oh, no, thought Hazel. This was the worst thing that could have happened! Michael Drummond was one of those showy Greville boys in her class at school. Why wasn't he down at the ships with everybody else?

She turned around and faced the other direction, hoping he wouldn't recognise her.

'Well, well! Hazel Green. Let me see what you're advertising.'

Hazel ignored him.

'Soap? Shampoo? I'm sure everyone at school will love to know!'

That was too much! 'I'm not advertising anything.'

'Not advertising anything?' Michael Drummond walked around and looked at the placard. He frowned for a moment, then shook his head.

Hazel grinned. He was just like everybody else.

'What are you laughing at?' he cried.

'You,' said Hazel. 'What are you doing here, anyway? Why aren't you down at the ships?'

'I'm ill.'

'What are you doing outside, then? You don't look ill.'

'I'm better now.'

'A real miracle,' said Hazel. Greville children were *so* delicate.

'At least I'm not standing in the street and advertising detergent.'

'I'm not *advertising*. I bet you don't even understand what's written there. You'd need more than forty-eight minutes to understand it, that's for sure.'

'Would not!'

'More like forty-eight hours.'

'You wait, Hazel Green! If you think you can just stand here in front of the Greville Building with an advertising sign . . . This isn't the Moodey Building.'

'Exactly! We don't have people like Mr X living in the Moodey Building.'

'Well . . . Mr X wouldn't *want* to live in the Moodey Building,' Michael shouted, beating his fists in the air. 'Just you wait! Just wait, Hazel Green.'

Hazel waited. It didn't take long. Michael ran inside and a moment later came back with a man who was wearing a peaked cap, just like the man who had been behind the counter at the Pollock Building, with a green blazer and tie.

'Look,' cried Michael, 'look what she's doing.'

'Calm down, Michael,' said the man. 'And let go of my arm.'

Hazel grinned. Greville children were *so* spoiled.

'Now, young lady—Michael, *let go*, I said! Now, young lady,' he began again, politely, 'we don't really allow people to advertise outside the Greville Building.'

Who was *we*, wondered Hazel, the association of men in peaked caps? Anyway, who was advertising?

'This isn't an advertisement,' she said.

'What is it, then?'

'It's a poem,' said Hazel. 'Ask anyone. Ask him, for instance,' she said, pointing to the Yak, who had returned by this time.

'It is a poem,' said the Yak. 'I helped write it.'

'Rubbish!' said Michael.

'It's true. How would you know, anyway?' said Hazel.

The man in the peaked cap sighed and shook his head. 'Let me read it.' He peered at the placard. 'It doesn't make any sense at all.'

That was really insulting. 'It makes plenty of sense! You just don't understand it.'

'Well, why don't you explain it to me?'

'I can't. That's the whole point.'

'Send them away!' cried Michael. 'Send them away!'

The man shook his head in exasperation. 'Look, I don't want to stop you showing your . . . poem. Why don't you just go down the street and do it?'

'There's a man in a sandwich down there who's got a patch. He'll take us to Benny's if we do that,' said Hazel.

'Yes,' added the Yak, 'and we don't even know where Benny's is.'

The man in the peaked cap shook his head in exasperation. Michael Drummond was still pulling at his arm, and he swatted at his hand to drive him away. A small crowd had gathered round to see what was happening. The man in the sandwich board came up to have a look as well. 'Come to Benny's,' he was whispering to people in the crowd, 'hamburgers for $2.50.'

'Well, either you go or I'll have to call the police,' said the man eventually. 'I'm sorry, but that's what I'll have to do.'

Michael Drummond sneered triumphantly.

'Go on, then,' said Hazel. 'Call the police.'

'You don't want me to call the police,' said the man. 'Really, it would be much better if you just left.'

Better for who, wondered Hazel. 'We do want you to call the police.'

'No we don't, Hazel,' whispered the Yak. 'Mathematicians don't—'

'What's wrong?' continued Hazel, speaking to the man. 'Scared?'

The man shook his head. 'All right, if that's what you want.'

'Yeah, if that's what you want!' said Michael Drummond.

'*Stop!*'

Everyone looked around.

'Stop it, *please*. This is terrible. Don't call the police.'

Hazel tried to see who had spoken. Out of the crowd stepped a lady in a brown coat and purple beret. Hazel had seen her before. She remembered her by the beret. She could remember seeing her coming out of the Greville Building some time during the morning. Later, Hazel thought, she had seen her watching from the other side of the street. And perhaps she had noticed her another time as well . . .

'Let me handle this, Jefferey.'

The man in the peaked cap looked at her doubtfully. 'Are you sure, Mrs Ehrlich?'

The lady nodded. 'Go away, now,' she called to the crowd of onlookers. 'Go on, there's nothing to see.'

'Yes,' cried Jefferey, 'it's all over now.'

'You too, Michael,' said Mrs Ehrlich. 'Off you go. Go on. No arguments from you.'

Michael gave Hazel one last, mocking glance. 'Wait until everyone hears about this!' he whispered, as Jefferey took his arm and dragged him away. The crowd dispersed. Finally only Mrs Ehrlich was left with Hazel and the Yak.

'Don't think you're going to make us go away,' said

Hazel. 'Jefferey will have to get the police first.'

Mrs Ehrlich shook her head. 'You've made a mistake,' she said.

'No, we know exactly what we're doing.'

'No, in your placard. It shouldn't say "nasty man". It should say "nasty woman".'

Hazel stared at Mrs Ehrlich. Her mouth dropped.

'Mr X?' she murmured disbelievingly.

'*Mrs* X, I think,' said the Yak.

So this was the person who had started it all!

20

'IN A WAY,' said Mrs Ehrlich, 'I'm glad you found me. I was wondering when it was going to happen.'

Hazel stared at her stonily. She had to keep reminding herself that underneath this sweet exterior and the funny purple beret was a hardened criminal who had stolen Mr Petrusca's lobsters and humiliated him with her note.

Mrs Ehrlich was taking off her coat. They were standing in the hallway of her apartment.

'That's a very nice jacket you're wearing, Yakov,' she said, as she took off her beret. 'And I like your tie as well.'

'Thank you,' said Yakov. 'It was for the detective work.'

A hardened criminal, thought Hazel, with a weird taste in clothes!

'Would you like something to drink?'

'Yes, please,' said Yakov.

'Hazel?'

Hazel didn't reply. She was pretty sure you weren't meant to take drinks from hardened criminals. She was pretty sure you weren't meant to give them your name, either, and it was only with great reluctance, after the Yak had already told her his, that she had muttered it to Mrs Ehrlich.

'Lemonade?'

'Yes, please,' said the Yak.

'Hazel?'

'All right,' said Hazel grudgingly, but that didn't mean she would actually drink it. If Mrs Ehrlich thought she was going to get off lightly by supplying lemonade, she was going to be disappointed.

Mrs Ehrlich disappeared and came back with a bottle and glasses. Then she led them into a room where there were two sofas. Hazel and the Yak sat on one and Mrs Ehrlich sat opposite them. There was a glass-topped table in between. Mrs Ehrlich poured the lemonade into three glasses and put them down on the table.

The Yak picked up his glass and drank. Mrs Ehrlich took a sip. But Hazel didn't touch hers.

'Oh, Hazel,' said Mrs Ehrlich, 'you don't look very pleased with me.'

Hazel didn't think that needed an answer.

'Well, I suppose I'd better tell you what happened.' Mrs Ehrlich sighed. She took another sip from her glass and put it down. Then she sat back and frowned in thought. 'Let me go back to the beginning. When Neville and I were much younger—'

'Neville?' said Hazel sharply.

'Neville Trimbel,' said Mrs Ehrlich.

'I see,' said Hazel, and she glanced at the Yak, as if this were an extremely important piece of evidence.

'Well, when we were much younger, Neville and I . . . well, we were more than ordinary friends.'

Of course, Hazel said to herself, now we're going to hear a sob story. That's always the way with hardened criminals, they'll say anything to get sympathy when they're cornered!

'In fact, Neville proposed to me. One night we went out for a wonderful lobster dinner, and as soon as we'd finished, he got down on his knees, and asked me to marry him. Oh . . .' sighed Mrs Ehrlich, 'what a wonderful memory. I'll never forget it. He looked so silly. He was so nervous he'd forgotten to take his lobster bib off!'

Mrs Ehrlich chuckled. The Yak grinned. Even Hazel had to struggle to keep a smile off her face.

'But I didn't marry him,' said Mrs Ehrlich. 'You see, I just didn't feel quite the same about him as he did about me. He was my dearest friend, but I'd fallen in love with someone else. It was him I married.'

'And I suppose you were dreadfully unhappy and we're all meant to feel sorry?' Hazel demanded impatiently.

'No, not at all,' said Mrs Ehrlich with surprise. 'What makes you say that? I was very happy. I had three lovely children. They're all grown up now. Look, you can see their pictures.'

Hazel and the Yak looked around. There were pictures

on the shelves behind them. Children and grandchildren as well!

'My husband, who was somewhat older than me, died seven years ago. But we had thirty-two wonderful years together.'

'That's not bad,' said the Yak calculating quickly. 'That means you spent 82.1% of your time together since you were married.'

'Really?' said Mrs Ehrlich.

'Of course, the percentage will decrease as time goes on.'

'Mrs Ehrlich, why are you telling us about your children and your husband?' said Hazel.

'I'll tell you why. After I married Eric, Neville knew we would never be together. But I made sure he knew that he was still the dearest friend I had, and there was no one else who could ever replace him. So although he was very sad that I said no, we always remained friends. And every year, on the anniversary of the day he proposed, we would meet together to have a lobster dinner, just so we would never forget how strong our friendship was. At first we met in a restaurant, then Neville started to make the dinners at home. He's quite a cook, you know.'

'He doesn't have much of a sense of humour,' muttered Hazel.

'No, that's true. He doesn't. Anyway, he began to make the meals at home. We bought the lobsters ourselves. In fact, we began to compete to see who could get the biggest and best ones. Neville and I always used to compete in everything, you see, ever since the first day we met at our cycling club. The lobster competition started off as a joke, of course, but somehow . . . it became very serious. Neville and I only know one way to compete—and that's as hard as we can. And Neville always won! *Always!* It drove me mad. There was just no way to beat him. For thirty years, he would always have better lobsters than mine. Mine looked like *shrimps* compared with his. When Eric was alive, he used to help me look for the best lobsters we could find, but even together we couldn't win. And then, last year, I finally found out why. Neville had always been careful not to say where he got his lobsters from. But last year he let it slip by mistake.' Mrs Ehrlich's voice dropped to a whisper. 'Petrusca's! The Fishmonger of Distinction. Of course, I'd tried Petrusca's, even bought lobsters there myself, and *still* they weren't as good as Neville's. Only then did I understand. Petrusca must have been getting him special ones—and feeding them up in the back!'

The Yak nodded. 'That would appear to be the most likely conclusion,' he said.

'So this year,' said Mrs Ehrlich, 'I came up with a plan. It was meant to be a joke—'

Hazel snorted.

'Honestly, Hazel. I was just going to go into Petrusca's, grab the lobsters and leave a note for Neville. When Mr

Petrusca gave it to him, Neville would immediately work out what had happened. Then we'd all laugh about it, because there was only one way to beat Neville at lobsters—and that was to cheat!' Mrs Ehrlich shook her head. 'But it all went wrong. Terribly wrong. I took the lobsters, there was no problem with that. It only took a couple of days of watching Mr Petrusca to work out how to do it. He always leaves his shop open when he goes to the café in the morning.'

'But that's at five o'clock!' cried Hazel. 'What were you doing up then?'

'Hazel, you don't understand how much I wanted to beat Neville. For thirty years he'd won. Even if it was only like this, only as a joke—I *had* to win! I would have done anything. I would have paid Petrusca ten times as much as Neville for those lobsters—'

'But he'd never have given them to you,' said Hazel.

'Exactly! So you see, I had no choice. The next morning, I lay in wait. As soon as I saw Petrusca cross the road to the café, I crept inside. I found the tank, grabbed the lobsters, stuffed them in a sack, left the note, and disappeared. It went like clockwork, just as I planned. The whole thing must have taken less than five minutes. Petrusca would have barely sat down to his coffee! I made a perfect getaway.'

Mrs Ehrlich paused. It was hard to imagine this sweet old lady dashing into the fishmonger's shop and pulling off such a daring robbery—but she had planned it to perfection.

'And then, everything went wrong. I sat here, waiting for Neville to call. Nothing! Not a word. Tomorrow, I thought. No, he didn't call then either. Three days went by, a week. I kept telling myself that any minute I'd hear the phone, but eventually I knew that I was fooling myself. Something had gone wrong.'

'And you didn't tell anyone? You just sat here?'

'Hazel, I felt like a fool. What had seemed so funny when I first thought about it suddenly seemed like a childish prank. A woman of my age! I'm a grandmother, for heaven's sake. If my little granddaughter Elsie had done that, I'd have told her to act her age—and she's only four! And every day I left it . . . the worse it got, the more foolish I felt, the harder it was to admit it to anyone.' Mrs Ehrlich shook her head in despair. She threw up her hands.

Hazel glanced at the Yak. He shook his head silently.

'Days went by . . . weeks,' Mrs Ehrlich continued. 'I started waiting for the police to come. After all, I'd *stolen* something! I'd never done such a thing. What had come over me? Every time I heard a knock on the door, I'd jump. When I heard a siren outside I'd rush to the window to see if they were coming for me. You see how guilty I was—and even then my pride wouldn't allow me to confess! I was so frightened of looking foolish. The day

171

before our dinner, Neville rang me. He said he hadn't been able to find any special lobsters. He said someone had told him a story about a theft, but he didn't believe it. He was very disappointed in his fishmonger. Can you imagine how I felt? Oh, I felt so bad. I said I was sick. I said I couldn't come for our meal. I *was* sick, that's how bad I felt. "But you'll win," he said. "I've only got a couple of ordinary ones." No, I was too sick. So we didn't even have our dinner this year. It's the first time we've missed it in thirty years! And if that wasn't enough—today I saw you with your placard. At first I tried to ignore it, but I kept coming back to look. I knew it was meant for me. When Jefferey said he was going to call the police, I couldn't pretend any longer. Is Petrusca sad? Is he really? He was always such a cheerful man. What have I done? You're right. I belong in the frying pan with the lobsters. That's the place for me!' Mrs Ehrlich shook her head, as if she couldn't understand how she had allowed herself to do what she did. Suddenly she looked up. 'What happened to the note?' she cried. 'Tell me that, children. What happened to the note? What went wrong?'

'Mrs Ehrlich, you gave the note to someone who can't—'

Hazel stopped just in time. The Yak was glancing at her fiercely.

'It's just . . .' Hazel tried to think. 'You see, that was the problem with your plan!' she exclaimed suddenly. 'What was going to happen if something went wrong with the note? You should have thought of *that*, Mrs Ehrlich.'

'I should have. You're right. I should have. But you found it, didn't you?'

'That's not the point, is it?' demanded Hazel.

Mrs Ehrlich shook her head, as if she felt so miserable that she didn't know *what* the point was any more. 'No, you're right. It's not.'

'What about the code, Mrs Ehrlich?' said the Yak. 'Why did you use that?'

'Oh, the code,' said Mrs Ehrlich, waving a hand. 'That was nothing. Neville and I always write to each other in code. It's another thing we compete in. And the poem, that's another thing. Every year, after he'd produced the best lobsters, he'd send me a little poem, giving me hints about how to get better lobsters next time. All these stupid competitions! Oh, what have I done? I missed out on my dinner with Neville for the first time in thirty years. I stole. I made the fishmonger unhappy. And all because I wanted to win a lobster competition! What kind of a grandmother am I? I'm so ashamed.'

Mrs Ehrlich began to cry. All the guilt and foolishness that had built up inside her burst out. She covered her face with her hands.

Hazel gazed at her. *What was going on?* Did adults really do things like that—play pranks on each other and feel foolish when they didn't work? That was the kind of thing she did with her friends! *Adults* weren't meant to do it. And did they really have competitions like that, to get the biggest lobsters or write the cleverest codes? And then there was Mr Petrusca, of course, who spent his whole life pretending to be able to do something he couldn't. That was *another* thing adults weren't supposed to do.

It was all very surprising. There had been quite a lot of surprises for Hazel since she began investigating this whole fishy business of the lobster theft—including the fishy way all these adults had been behaving. She was starting to feel more grown up than a number of the so-called grown-ups around her! That was perhaps the biggest surprise of all, and Hazel wasn't sure whether she liked it.

Meanwhile, it was impossible to think of Mrs Ehrlich as a hardened criminal, or even as a softened criminal . . . or any kind of criminal at all. She hadn't meant to hurt anyone, and her plan would have been quite funny—*if* it had worked.

'Look,' whispered Hazel, leaning towards Mrs Ehrlich to see if she could cheer her up, 'Yakov's playing the violin.'

Mrs Ehrlich took her hands away from her face.

'Where?'

'There,' whispered Hazel. 'He plays it in his head. He's probably playing something slow and sad.'

Mrs Ehrlich looked at her questioningly. 'That's very peculiar.'

'Yes,' said Hazel, 'the Yak's a very peculiar boy.' And she picked up her glass and took a drink of her lemonade, as they both watched the Yak playing a melody in his head.

'There's just one other thing,' said Hazel eventually, after Mrs Ehrlich had pulled out a handkerchief and dried her eyes. 'What happened to the lobsters?'

'That's almost the worst part of it!' cried Mrs Ehrlich, loud enough to disturb the Yak's playing and make him look up with a start. 'Come and I'll show you.'

Mrs Ehrlich led them out of the room and down the hallway. She opened a door.

'Look!' she said, throwing out an arm.

Hazel and the Yak looked. It was Mrs Ehrlich's bathroom. The bath was full of water. And there, at the bottom, were two enormous lobsters, as big and as angry as they had been when Hazel had last seen them . . . in Mr Petrusca's tank!

21

THE TWO PRIZE lobsters moved around the bottom of the bath, crashing into each other and clashing with their claws.

'I just didn't know what to do with them,' said Mrs Ehrlich. 'I felt so guilty, I couldn't even eat them. And if you know how much I love lobsters, you'll know how guilty that is! I just left them there.'

'You've kept them here all this time?' said Hazel, grinning, and she went closer and knelt down to look at the lobsters, which rose up and snapped as soon as they saw her shadow over the bath.

Mrs Ehrlich nodded. 'I've been feeding them every day. What appetites they have. I've never bought so much fish! They seem to like sea bass the most. Oh, but it's been awful, Hazel. Every time I want a bath I have to put them in the basin. And they bite!'

She rolled up her sleeve, and her forearms were covered in red marks where the lobsters had snapped her.

Hazel laughed. The Yak laughed as well. Mrs Ehrlich couldn't help chuckling, even as she rubbed the bruises on her arms.

'So what should I do?' she said.

Hazel turned to face Mrs Ehrlich. Suddenly she felt very grown-up again, as if Mrs Ehrlich were not many years older than her, but many years younger, and had to be told what needed to be done.

'Well,' said Hazel seriously, after she had given it some thought, 'the first thing is, I think you should give the lobsters back to Mr Petrusca. And then . . . I think you should explain everything that happened.'

'Everything?' said Mrs Ehrlich.

'Yes,' said Hazel. 'No matter how foolish it makes you feel. And *then* I think you should apologise to him.'

'Yes, I certainly need to apologise to him.'

'And I think you should explain everything to Neville, and ask him to apologise as well. Because when Mr Petrusca said the lobsters had been stolen, they really *had* been stolen, and Neville should have believed him.'

'Yes,' said Mrs Ehrlich.

'But there's one other thing,' Hazel said suddenly. 'When I said to tell Mr Petrusca *everything*, I didn't mean about the note. You shouldn't mention that. Don't ask if Mr Petrusca found it, or if he read it, or *what* he did with it.'

Mrs Ehrlich frowned.

'Make her swear on her nose,' whispered the Yak.

'Do you promise, Mrs Ehrlich?'

'But I don't see why—'

'Mr Petrusca is very sensitive about the note. You can

177

tell Neville about it, but he has to promise not to mention it as well. In fact, you've both got to promise not to mention it to anyone else—not only to Mr Petrusca, but to *anyone* at all. You'll ruin everything if you do. Just say you took the lobsters as a joke, and you're very sorry.'

'But surely Mr Petrusca will ask about the note?'

Hazel shook her head. 'He *won't* ask. And you mustn't mention it. If you do you'll just make it worse. *Pretend* it never existed.'

Mrs Ehrlich gazed at Hazel for a moment. She nodded. 'All right. I can't say I've acted very intelligently so far. If that's what you suggest, that's what I'll do.'

Hazel nodded. 'And another thing. You don't have to tell Mr Petrusca about me or Yakov.'

'Oh, but Hazel, I'll want him to know what good friends you are. Not everyone has friends who would do what you—'

'Please, Mrs Ehrlich. Just say you felt so guilty, and so ashamed, that you had to apologise.'

'Well, I did feel guilty . . .'

'And ashamed.'

'Yes, and ashamed.'

'Just tell him that. That's perfect.'

It *was* perfect. Hazel was sure that Mrs Gluck would have agreed. All the other punishments that Hazel had thought up—like making the culprit go to the fish market at two o'clock in the morning for a month—

didn't compare. To be ashamed was the perfect punishment for someone who had made someone *else* feel ashamed, even if they hadn't realised they were doing it. And the funny thing was that it was Mrs Ehrlich who had punished herself, without anyone else's help.

'All right,' said Mrs Ehrlich, 'that's what I'll do. I'll go tomorrow.'

'Tomorrow's Sunday.'

'Well, I'll go on Monday. I won't leave it a day longer!'

'Hazel,' said the Yak, as they were walking back, 'do you realise you were going to get us arrested?'

Hazel shook her head. 'I was *not* going to get us arrested. Jefferey wasn't going to call the police. People always say things like that, but they never actually do it.'

'He looked like the kind of person who'd do it.'

'Even if he had called the police—which is very unlikely—we'd have had plenty of time to leave before they got there.'

'I have to tell you, Hazel,' the Yak said seriously, 'you asked me to help solve a mathematical problem. I don't expect to be arrested for it.'

'You were never going to be—'

The Yak stopped. 'Swear!' he said. 'Swear on your nose!'

'What?'

'That you'll never get me arrested for working on a mathematical problem.'

'Oh, that's ridiculous.'

'I know. Now do it, Hazel Green,' said the Yak, who had never had anything to make her swear about before.

'Really, Yakov. It doesn't mean anything to you.'

'But you make me do it all the time.'

'Yes, because it means something to *me*.'

Yakov waited. For a mathematician, thought Hazel, he wasn't being particularly logical.

Hazel shrugged. 'All right,' she said. She put her finger on her nose and swore.

'Good,' said the Yak, grinning, as if that alone had made the whole afternoon worthwhile.

Hazel laughed. If it made the Yak happy, she would have sworn on her ears and her eyes as well. By this time on Monday, the lobsters would have been returned to their rightful tank in the back of the fish shop. Mr Petrusca would have received the apology he deserved. And then, he really could forget about the whole episode. For Hazel, *that* was what really mattered.

But there was something else that mattered as well—or if it didn't matter at that moment, it soon would. By this time on Monday, Hazel would have had to walk to school with twenty other people who had all expected her to be with them on Saturday—and who were going to want an explanation!

22

MONDAY MORNING WAS a nightmare. *Everyone* demanded to know why Hazel hadn't come to the ships. More importantly, everyone seemed to have his or her own explanation, which had to be shouted up and down the street . . . and they weren't particularly complimentary.

Well, thought Hazel, when she finally arrived at the school gate, things couldn't possibly get worse.

Wrong. In the morning, no one knew where she had been on Saturday. By the time they walked home in the afternoon, everyone had heard the story from Michael Drummond—or at least, the story Michael Drummond decided to tell. According to him, she had been standing outside the Greville Building with the Yak . . . advertising detergent. Five police had come to arrest her and she was already in handcuffs before she was saved by a nosy old lady.

'I was *not* arrested. And I was *not* advertising detergent.'

'What were you advertising? Deodorant?'

Hazel didn't reply. She wasn't going to say anything else. If she started explaining, she knew, everything would come out, and it was a secret. It had to stay a secret.

She bit her lip and marched stonily ahead while the others shouted, laughed and poked fun all around her.

'Let's get Hazel to advertise dog food—'

'We'll call it Hazel Mush—'

'Or cat food—'

'Hazel Mouse—'

'I know! I know!' shouted Leon Davis. 'Let's get her to advertise *Yak food*.'

Everyone laughed.

'What do yaks eat?'

'Grass!'

'Seeds!'

'Potatoes!'

'Weeds!'

'Violin strings!'

That got the biggest laugh of all. Hazel kept going. She stared ahead and marched as fast as she could. But it wasn't fast enough. The noise rose all around her. Everyone kept shouting. She sealed her lips and pressed them together tighter and tighter, to stop from speaking. How much easier it would have been to tell them what had actually happened. She had vowed to catch a thief, and she had done it! What was wrong with that? All she had to do was tell them . . . and not one of them would shout at her again.

Hazel was discovering something: silence is hard, much harder than speech. But she wouldn't give in. She had started the day with Mr Petrusca's secret and she was going to end the day with it!

No one had ever seen Hazel Green respond like that before. She always gave as good as she got—and you could usually count on something extra as well! Her silence made everyone want to attack her even more.

'How about *Yak soap*? She could advertise that!'

'Or *Yak flea powder!*'

'Yeah, *fleas! Fleas!*' yelled Robert Fischer, bouncing around and shouting in her ear.

'*Fleas!*' cried Paul Boone, scratching at Hazel's neck. Someone scratched at her arm . . . at her back . . . '*Fleas! Fleas!*' She felt hands at her face. People were shouting. Someone was pulling her satchel. Someone was pulling her hair. She threw out her arms. Someone twisted her fingers.

Someone flew across in front of her.

Suddenly there was silence. Paul Boone was sprawled on the ground.

'Stop it!' said the person who had knocked him over. 'That's enough!'

Everyone had stopped, watching in amazement. It was Marcus Bunn!

Hazel was as surprised as anyone. Marcus was so jealous of the Yak that when they had started walking home he was poking fun as much as the rest of them.

Paul Boone picked himself up off the ground, gazing at Marcus in disbelief.

Marcus's face was red. His eyes flashed behind his glasses. He stood in front of Hazel, as if he were going to protect her from everybody else. That was the most astonishing thing of all. Marcus was always the last to join in a fight, and he never joined in at all if he couldn't find someone to hold his glasses.

'Go on,' he said. 'Go home!'

'Oh, *Marcus,*' simpered Leon Davis. 'I didn't know we were hurting your *feelings.*'

'Yeah, I didn't know—'

But Marcus stood his ground. 'Go on! Go home, all of you! That's enough.'

There was no reason for everyone to listen to Marcus. After all, there were so many of them that they could easily have taken him out of the way.

But there was silence. Maybe, now that everyone wasn't shouting, they were starting to feel foolish at the things they had said, or maybe it was simply the surprise of seeing Marcus take a stand that made them think again.

After a minute, a couple of people moved away. Others followed. Even Leon Davis left without another word. Robert Fischer pulled a face and ran after him. Finally only Hazel and Marcus remained.

'Well?' said Marcus.

'Well what?'

'You could *thank* me.'

'I don't need *you* to protect me, Marcus. You already told me not to expect any help from you.'

'Well, you weren't helping yourself. They were going to kill you.'

'Nonsense,' said Hazel. 'I had them exactly where I wanted them. I was using a new technique, that's all.'

'Really? What was that?'

'Silence. It was working quite well until you spoiled it.'

Marcus stared at her angrily. 'Thanks a lot, Hazel!' he said, and he turned and stomped away.

Hazel watched him for a moment. She grinned. Then she ran to catch up with him.

'Marcus?'

Marcus didn't reply. He was too busy stomping away in a huff.

'Marcus!'

Hazel reached out for his arm. Marcus shook her away. Hazel grabbed him.

'What?' he demanded. 'What is it?'

'I just wanted to say something.'

'What?'

'Thanks.'

Marcus folded his arms across his chest. He narrowed his eyes suspiciously.

'I mean it, Marcus. Silence isn't much of a defence. Don't try it unless you have to.'

'I still can't tell you what I was doing on Saturday,' Hazel said as they walked home.

'Why not?'

'I just can't, Marcus.'

Marcus nodded. 'Well, I didn't really expect you to. If you couldn't tell me on Saturday, there's no reason why you should be able to tell me today.'

True, thought Hazel. Marcus was very fair sometimes.

'And I can't tell you why the Yak was helping me.'

Marcus frowned. 'Hazel,' he said, and then he hesitated for a moment. 'Hazel, sometimes I think . . . well, it's just . . . sometimes I think you like the Yak more than me.'

'Really? I never imagined you thought that. What makes you say so?'

'Well, sometimes you go and visit him instead of doing things with me.'

'And sometimes I do things with you instead of going to visit him. Have you ever thought about that?'

'No,' said Marcus. 'I haven't.'

'You should.'

Marcus grinned.

They were close to home.

'Anyway, it's all finished now,' said Hazel, 'the thing I had to do on Saturday. The job's done.'

'That's good,' said Marcus.

'I'm sorry I missed the ships. What were they like, anyway?'

'Oh, they were all right. We didn't get to go on them. They were all closed off. Then the Grevillers and the Burbankers got in a fight, and we all watched them and laughed.'

'So it was fun, then?'

'Well, they only had a scuffle, really. It could have been better. There were lots of sailors around and everyone was frightened of them. They *really* know how to fight.'

Hazel stopped in front of the flower shop. 'Come on, let's go and see Mrs Gluck.'

Marcus pulled a face. 'Flowers aren't for boys.'

'Of course they are,' said Hazel. 'You love them.' And she pushed him inside.

23

MRS GLUCK WAS working on a centrepiece for the Firemen's Association spring ball. It took up the whole length of the worktable, and at the centre it rose to almost a metre in height. The Fire Chief wanted more than three hundred flowers. He was going to send four of his men in a truck to pick it up.

The arrangement was full of burning reds and fiery oranges. That was what the firemen wanted. Not a single cool white or calming purple. Hazel thought this was very strange. Surely they saw enough hot colours when they were at work!

Marcus was watching with fascination. He hardly blinked. He had never seen such a large arrangement.

'I saw Mrs Volio today,' said Mrs Gluck, her head hidden behind the arrangement as she slotted some delicate red rosebuds into it.

'Which one?' said Hazel.

'Young Mrs Volio. She came in for some lilies. She told me Mr Petrusca's lobsters have turned up.'

'Really?' said Hazel.

'Yes, apparently so,' said Mrs Gluck. 'A lady called Mrs Erfurt just walked—'

'Erfurt? Are you sure it wasn't Ehrlich?'

'Yes,' said Mrs Gluck, looking at Hazel over the arrangement. 'Why do you ask?'

'Well, I'm just . . . it's just . . . Erfurt's a funny name, that's all.'

'Well, this Mrs Erfurt, or whatever her name is, just walked in with the two lobsters in a sack. Apparently she's Mr Trimbel's friend, and it was she who'd taken them. She apologised, of course. So did Mr Trimbel, who was with her.'

'Isn't that who you were looking for, Hazel?' said Marcus Bunn. 'Mr Trimbel's fr—'

Hazel gave Marcus a quick elbow in the ribs. Mrs Gluck raised her eyebrows.

'Did Mr Petrusca seem happy?' said Hazel.

'Apparently he did. When Mrs Volio went to see him, he was singing at the top of his voice. A song about filleting fish, I think.'

Hazel grinned.

'And to show how sorry they are, Mrs Erfurt and Mr Trimbel have invited Mr and Mrs Petrusca to a special dinner. A special *lobster* dinner.'

'Quite right,' said Hazel. 'It's the least they can do.'

Suddenly Mrs Gluck put down the flower in her hands and looked at Hazel. 'And are you telling me, *Hazel Green*, that you had nothing to do with this?'

Marcus Bunn suddenly looked up at her as well, as if he

were very interested to find out.

'Well . . . I . . . I didn't say I had *nothing* to do with it,' stammered Hazel. Then she frowned, trying to remember exactly what she had said. 'Did I?'

Mrs Gluck smiled. 'No, you didn't.'

'You didn't,' said Marcus.

Mrs Gluck waited. Hazel was silent. If there was one person in the world who wouldn't make her talk about something if she didn't want to, it was Mrs Gluck.

'Well, I don't want to make you talk about it if you don't want to. All I *will* say is, if you ask me, a person ought to finish a job once they start it.'

And as if to prove that she meant what she said, Mrs Gluck picked up an orange chrysanthemum and poked it into the arrangement.

But Hazel didn't know *what* she meant! Finish the job? What was there left to finish?

'Isn't Mr Petrusca happy now?' she asked.

'I think so,' said Mrs Gluck. 'At least, he was singing!'

'And hasn't he got his lobsters back?' asked Hazel.

Mrs Gluck nodded, stabbing another chrysanthemum into the arrangement opposite the first.

'And haven't Mrs Ehrlich and Mr Trimbel apologised?'

'Yes,' said Mrs Gluck, 'I believe they have.'

'Then I don't understand, Mrs Gluck.'

Mrs Gluck put down her flowers again. She shook her head. She glanced at Marcus. 'What do you think, Marcus?'

Marcus shrugged. He had no idea.

'Hazel Green,' said Mrs Gluck, 'sometimes I think you're the cleverest girl I've ever met . . . And sometimes you don't seem to see the one thing that's as obvious as the nose on your face.'

Hazel frowned. Suddenly her nose felt itchy, and she scratched.

'Listen,' said Mrs Gluck, 'was it really those two lobsters that made Mr Petrusca so unhappy? Was it really the fact that someone had stolen them? Was that what this was all about? No, it wasn't. It was something else, wasn't it?'

'That was a *secret*, Mrs Gluck!' whispered Hazel, glancing anxiously at Marcus. She whispered: 'How do you know about that? I didn't tell you, did I?'

Mrs Gluck shook her head.

'Don't tell me the Yak told you. I told *him* about it. I had to, otherwise he wouldn't have done all the code work. But he wouldn't tell anyone, not the Yak.'

'I've never even met Yakov,' said Mrs Gluck. 'I've asked you before to bring him down to me.'

'He only goes to places where there are mathematical problems.'

'He hardly goes *anywhere*,' added Marcus. 'That's why

Hazel always has to visit his apartment.'

'Well, I'm sure we can find a mathematical problem for him here. There must be one somewhere!' said Mrs Gluck.

They all looked around the workroom, as if there *must* be a mathematical problem—at least one—floating in one of the vases or hiding under a flower.

'How did you find out?' said Hazel, turning back to Mrs Gluck.

'Sometimes there are things you just . . . know. It doesn't really matter how I found out, Hazel. What matters is what you're going to do about it. Nothing's really changed, has it?' Mrs Gluck paused. 'What's to stop it happening again?'

Hazel glanced at Marcus. Then she leaned forward to whisper. Marcus leaned forward as well.

'But he needs a teacher!'

'True.'

'Someone who really cares about him and wants to help him find the right way to learn.'

'Yes,' said Mrs Gluck. 'I wonder who that would be?'

Hazel left Mrs Gluck's shop deep in thought. She didn't even glance at Sophie, who was arranging the bouquets that she had just arranged an hour before.

When she was outside she said: 'I'm sorry, Marcus, there's something I have to do.'

'I know. You can't tell me, can you?'

Hazel shook her head. 'You know that job I said was finished on Saturday? Well, it looks like there's something left to do.'

24

THE YAK'S MOTHER opened the door. Today, there was not a trace of colour about her. She wore a white silk gown, and her fingernails were painted white as well. Her shoes and her hair were black. In her hand she held a necklace of black and white porcelain beads.

Hazel frowned.

'Well?'

Hazel nodded. Yes, why not?

'Yes,' said the Yak's mother, 'that's what I think.'

'And you could wear a pair of sunglasses as well, with black lenses and white frames,' said Hazel, and the Yak's mother was so surprised at the suggestion, or fascinated by it, that she stood there thinking while Hazel walked past her and went to find the Yak in his room.

The Yak was sitting at his desk, scribbling calculations in front of an open book.

'Solved it?' she said.

The Yak looked around with a start. 'How did you get in?'

'I climbed up the outside of the building with my bare hands, opened one of your windows with my fingernails, and . . . here I am!'

Hazel bounced onto the Yak's bed and sat there watching him with a grin.

'You didn't really do that, did you?'

'No, I actually let myself down from the roof with a rope, drilled through the wall—'

'Very funny,' said the Yak.

Hazel shrugged. 'People usually get the answers they ask for,' she said, which is what her grandmother often told her. 'But it's not always the answer they want!'

The Yak thought about that. 'If that's true, then all you need to do is work out your question carefully enough in the first place, and then you're sure to hear what you'd like.'

But it *wasn't* true, thought Hazel. It was just something her grandmother liked to say. Very few of her grandmother's sayings were true, at least, they were never *always* true.

'Yakov,' said Hazel, 'I've got a question.'

The Yak narrowed his eyes suspiciously. Hazel's questions had a habit of turning into answers he *didn't* want.

'What do you think it takes to teach something to somebody?'

'Oh, no, Hazel, if you think I'm going to start teaching you mathematics, you can just stop right there! That problem of yours with Mr Trimbel and Mrs Ehrlich wasn't a real mathematical problem at all. I've been thinking about it and there are at least six reasons it isn't. Listen, I'll tell you them. First—'

'No, I wasn't thinking of mathematics.'

The Yak sighed with relief.

'I was thinking more of the violin!'

'Hazel, I could never teach you the violin,' cried the Yak. 'To learn the violin takes patience. It takes time. It takes . . .'

Hazel stopped listening. If there were six reasons against the Trimbel-Ehrlich problem, there must be at least eight reasons against her learning the violin, and since she didn't want to learn the violin anyway, she wasn't really interested in hearing them. It was funny, though, how she had asked a simple question and the Yak had immediately assumed it would mean some kind of work for him. When did she *ever* ask him to do anything?

'Finished?' said Hazel, when the Yak had finally fallen silent, facing her with his arms crossed firmly in front of his chest.

'No, it takes a violin, as well. And you're not touching mine!'

Hazel sighed. 'Oh, well, I suppose I'll have to give up that idea, then. Perhaps you can actually answer my question now.'

The Yak frowned. 'I have answered your question. I'm not teaching you the violin and that's that.'

'I didn't ask you to teach me. I asked you what you

thought it takes to be able to teach something to someone else. Remember?'

'Ye-e-es . . .' said the Yak suspiciously, wondering what Hazel was up to now.

'That's it. What do you think?'

'Teach someone what? Mathematics?'

'If you like. Or it could be something else. Geography, for example.'

'Well, I think you just have to . . .' the Yak paused, really thinking. 'I think you have to understand the principles. Like with mathematics, if you're solving a problem, and you've got two unknowns, you have to understand the principle of getting the first unknown, which will then help you get the second.'

'Unless it's Mr Trimbel,' Hazel pointed out.

'And then,' said the Yak, ignoring Hazel's remark, 'you have to know the details. For example, how can you find the first unknown? What are the mathematical operations you can do to find it?'

'What about geography?'

'Well, there might be a principle . . .' The Yak paused to think. 'All right, here's an example. Rivers get bigger as they approach the sea, because of the increasing volume of water they carry. That's a geographical principle.'

'Do they get bigger? I didn't know that.'

'We learned it last week, Hazel!'

'We didn't learn it last week. We were obviously taught

it last week. You don't remember the things you're taught, Yakov, only the things you learn,' Hazel said knowledgeably. That was another one of her grandmother's sayings, which was sometimes true, like now, for instance.

The Yak shook his head. 'If that's the principle, *then* there are the details about specific rivers. How much water do they carry? How wide are they when they reach the sea? Take the Morangie, for instance.'

The *Morangie*? Where was it, anyway? It sounded like some kind of cake. Surely the Yak wasn't going to tell her how wide the Morangie was when it reached the sea!

'Eight hundred and sixty metres,' said the Yak, 'at its mouth.'

The Yak smiled. Hazel wondered if the Yak just made these things up, because nobody else would know anyway. But she only wondered for a second, because on a shelf just above the Yak's head, Hazel noticed, was an atlas, and the reason she noticed it was that the Yak himself had turned to look at it, almost as if he could tell exactly what she was thinking . . . and was just *waiting* for her to say she didn't believe him.

'So,' said Hazel, 'principles and details?'

She looked at the Yak's violin stand beside the window. A book of music lay open. The musical notes ran across the page like dense hedges of sticks and blobs. How could you ever learn to interpret something like that? Principles and details? Somehow the Yak made it sound perfectly ordered. Of course, you could always see the details yourself. You could measure the width of a river. But . . .

'How do they get the principles?' said Hazel, thinking *that* would stump him.

'That's the whole point,' said the Yak enthusiastically. 'The principles come *from* the details. After hundreds of people have worked on something for years and years, collecting all sorts of details, you can start to see what the principles are. And then, when you *use* the principles, you start to discover more details . . .'

'And that gives you more principles?'

'Yes, yes!' cried the Yak.

'But then . . . it's just like a big circle! Where does it start? Where does it end? Principles . . . details . . . details . . . principles . . .'

'Exactly. That's the beauty of it. A circle. A perfect circle, always expanding, always growing, but always perfectly round. Knowledge is like a circle!'

It sounded a little bit *too* perfect to Hazel. 'There must be gaps. There must be bits missing.'

'Yes,' said the Yak. 'But those gaps can be filled, Hazel. And if you know they can be filled—*will* be filled, one day—then the circle's still there, even if the line isn't yet complete. It's *virtually* a circle.'

Hazel thought about this. Incomplete circles, lines with gaps? She wasn't sure what they were even talking about any more.

She tried to remember where they had started from.

'So, it's principles and details, you think?'

The Yak nodded. He had his smug mathematician-cat smile on his face again.

'You're wrong, of course.'

'No, I'm not.'

'You are,' said Hazel. What the Yak didn't realise was that he had a strange habit of being both right *and* wrong at the same time. He always seemed to know one part of the answer, but ignored another; he always chose the ordered bit and left out the part that was chaotic. Hazel, on the other hand, loved the chaotic and sometimes couldn't even be bothered with the ordered. 'What about finding ways to help the person you're teaching, and understanding the way they learn, getting to know them, just *wanting* to teach them? Everyone's different. What about all of that, Yakov?'

The Yak shrugged. 'Principles and details,' he said.

'Helping and understanding,' said Hazel.

'Principles and details!'

'Helping and understanding!'

They stared at each other. Eventually, the Yak said, very quietly, 'Maybe it's both.'

Hazel grinned. 'Exactly. Order *and* chaos, Yakov Plonsk.'

The Yak shook his head. But after a second he couldn't

keep a pointy, scrunched-up grin off his face.

'And anyone can do it? Anyone can teach anything if they do this?'

'I don't know if *anyone* can do it,' said the Yak. 'But they can try.'

25

HAZEL GOT INTO the elevator. She went straight up to her apartment. She went straight to her room. She opened the cupboard where she threw all her old exercise books and school books and other stuff she had finished with. She searched feverishly. She didn't even pause to answer when her mother called out to ask what she was looking for. Finally she found the book she wanted. Lucky she hadn't taken it to the Rum Warehouse to sell as an antique! She opened it on her lap and leafed through it. It was so babyish, she thought. She'd be ashamed to put it in front of a grown man . . .

No! That was exactly the problem. If *she* were ashamed, Mr Petrusca would be ashamed as well. But if she *weren't*, then he'd have no reason to be embarrassed either.

She ran out of the apartment with the book and pressed for the elevator again. Her heart was pounding. Thoughts were racing through her head. Principles? Details? Did she know enough? Would she be able to teach? When the elevator reached the ground floor, she still hadn't answered those questions. There was only one way to find out!

She reached Mr Petrusca's shop. She pushed the door open.

Mr Petrusca greeted her with a big smile. 'Hazel!' he cried. His hands were racing as he slit, gutted and filleted a fish, as fast as she had ever seen him do it.

He handed the fish over to a customer and came to talk to her.

'Did you know I got my lobsters back?'

'Yes.'

'It was just a joke. See? No harm done.'

'I know,' said Hazel. 'When will you be finished in the shop, Mr Petrusca?'

'In about half an hour.'

'Can I wait for you?'

Mr Petrusca gave her a puzzled look. 'If you like. Sit in the back. I'll try to be quicker.'

Hazel went and sat in the desk at the back of the shop. The two giant lobsters were back in their tank and Hazel looked at them while she waited. Mrs Petrusca and the assistants came in and out a couple of times, getting fish for customers. They all smiled at her.

Eventually Mr Petrusca came in. He took off his white fishmonger's apron and sat next to Hazel.

'What is it, Hazel? You know, if ever you want anything from me, you only have to ask. I'll never forget how kind you were when I was so unhappy.'

'I do want something from you, Mr Petrusca.'

'What? Name it! Even if I have to buy it for you, I'll get it. It doesn't matter how much it costs.'

'It's not something you can buy, Mr Petrusca. It's something you have to do yourself. And I don't think it will be easy, so you've got to promise to try.'

Mr Petrusca gazed silently at Hazel. He didn't understand.

'Mr Petrusca, you got the lobsters back, but our job isn't finished.'

'What do you mean?'

Hazel took the book from under her arm and laid it on the desk. Mr Petrusca glanced at it and then looked back at Hazel with a puzzled expression.

'It's my first-grade reader, Mr Petrusca. This is the book I learned to read from.'

Mr Petrusca started shaking his head. 'No, Hazel, I'm too old for this.'

Hazel opened the book. The first page showed a cat. It was a very childish drawing, something that five-year-olds would have liked to look at. Underneath it were the letters of the word, at first separately, and then all together.

'That's the letter C,' said Hazel, pointing at the first letter. 'That's one of the details you have to learn. There are a lot of others as well. But first, I have to tell you a principle, Mr Petrusca. Each letter has a sound. To make a word, you put the sounds of the letters together.'

'Hazel,' said Mr Petrusca. 'I'm a grown man. Look at this book.' He leafed through the pages. 'Cats, and dogs . . . and little boys . . . and kites. How can I learn from such a book?'

'Are you ashamed?' said Hazel.

'Yes, I'm ashamed!' said Mr Petrusca. 'I told you before. Why do you have to ask again?'

'I'll tell you why,' said Hazel suddenly, and quite fiercely. 'Because I'm *not*! I'd be more ashamed if I had to pretend all the time. Now you listen to me, Mr Petrusca,' she continued, not giving him even a moment to reply. 'There's a principle you have to learn and I'm going to teach it to you. Words are made by putting the sounds of the letters together. Here's C and it sounds like *kkk*, and here's T and it sound like *ttt*, and they're at the beginning and the end of the word *kkkattt*. Do you understand?'

Mr Petrusca stared at her in surprise.

Hazel explained again, pointing to the letters. Now Mr Petrusca was following her finger.

'But how do you know it's not kkkittt' he said, 'or . . . kkkottt?'

'Because,' said Hazel, 'see that letter there. That's A. And it gives an *aaa* sound. *Kkkk aaa tttt! Cat.*'

'*Kkkaaattt.*'

'Exactly. Now look,' she said, turning over the next page, 'here's exactly the same word, but the first letter has changed. Can you see?'

Mr Petrusca nodded, gazing at the page.

'It's a B. *Bbb*. Now, what do you think this word is? Remember, everything else is the same.'

Mr Petrusca frowned in concentration. He frowned so hard that it was almost painful to watch him. *'Bbbaaattt.'*

'Yes!' cried Hazel, jumping up in her excitement. 'Bat!'

'Bat!' cried Mr Petrusca, jumping up as well.

'Bat!' . . . *'Bat!'* . . . *'Bat!'* . . . *'Bat!'* they cried, joining hands and dancing around the room.

The two giant lobsters turned in their tank to watch them.

'Bat!' . . . *'Bat!'*

'Bat?'

Mr Petrusca froze. Mrs Petrusca was standing in the doorway to the shop.

'Where's a bat?'

Mr Petrusca went white. Hazel let go of him. She had never seen the colour drain away from someone so quickly.

'There aren't any bats,' he whispered, in a voice so small you wouldn't have thought it could even have come from a mouse.

'Yes, there are,' said Hazel.

Mrs Petrusca came into the room. She glanced at the book that lay open on the table.

'What are you doing, John?' she asked quietly.

Mr Petrusca was silent. He glanced at Hazel, frowning,

as if he were in pain, as if something inside him were tearing itself free, something that had been hidden for years and years and years as far deep inside his soul as he could bury it.

'I'm not ashamed,' Hazel whispered.

Mr Petrusca nodded. He looked up at his wife.

'I'm learning to read.'